A KNIGHTS BRIDGE
CHRISTMAS

CARLA NEGGERS

A KNIGHTS BRIDGE
CHRISTMAS

For Leo and Oona

PROLOGUE
➜❦

"I cannot change! I cannot! It's not that
I'm impenitent, it's just... Wouldn't it be
better if I just went home to bed?"

—CHARLES DICKENS, *A CHRISTMAS CAROL*

December, 1945

FIFTEEN-YEAR-OLD DAISY BLANCHARD
paused on South Main Street and sighed at the once-
stately house across from the Knights Bridge common,
just past the town library. Built in 1892, the house had a
curving front porch, tall windows and Victorian details
that must have looked grand in their day. Now, a week
before Christmas, the house looked shabby and forlorn

against the gray winter sky. It wasn't decorated. There wasn't so much as a wreath on the front door.

It was, by far, the worst-looking house in the village.

My house, Daisy thought with dismay.

Even through the war, she and her mother had managed to decorate for Christmas. They would scour the house for bits of ribbon and yarn and they would cut evergreen boughs and gather pinecones in the yard. They'd learned to be resourceful. Everyone in their small town west of Boston had done the same—using, reusing, mending, sharing what they had. Other homes, businesses, churches, the library and town offices were decorated for the season. The First Congregational Church had a crèche, and a family of carrot-nosed, top-hatted snowmen greeted shoppers at the country store.

The only reason her house wasn't decorated, Daisy knew, was because her father believed decorating was a waste of time and effort.

He was another Ebenezer Scrooge.

She felt bad for such thinking. *Give him time*, her mother had told her. Daisy was trying but it wasn't easy when she so desperately wanted to have fun this Christmas. For more than three years, her father had been away at war, serving in the navy in the Atlantic. She'd missed him so much. When he'd come home in September, she'd been so excited. But he'd changed during the war, and so had she. She'd grown up. She wasn't a child anymore. She couldn't explain the changes in him, except that fighting the war and being away had taken a toll. He didn't talk about his experience, but she knew he must have seen terrible things.

With the end of the war, the people of Knights Bridge were in the mood to throw off their worries and sadness and celebrate, if with a deep sense of appreciation for the sacrifices especially of those who had given their lives. When her father frustrated her—which was often these days—Daisy tried to remember how grateful she was he'd come home safe and sound. That wasn't the case for so many.

She heard someone behind her and turned, surprised to see Tom Farrell running down the library steps. He would never consider the steps might be icy. He had a stack of books in one arm. He was a senior, and he would be the first in his family to graduate from high school. He wanted to be a firefighter. He was already a volunteer firefighter. Given the books in his arms, Daisy knew he would have at least one report due for school, and he would be late. It was always the same. Somehow, though, he would turn in his work in the nick of time.

He grinned as he caught up with her. "Hi, Daisy." He spoke in that easygoing, confident way that was uniquely Tom Farrell. "I saw you in the library but I was too far away to say hello. I didn't want to shout and risk getting thrown out."

"I didn't see you."

"I'm doing a report on Charles Dickens for English class. I decided to read *A Christmas Carol* because it's short." He spoke cheerfully, moving his arm slightly so Daisy could see that, indeed, he had a copy of the Charles Dickens story with him. "That's the one about Scrooge, isn't it?"

"It is. Ebenezer Scrooge. He's visited by three spirits on Christmas Eve."

Tom shrugged, obviously not concerned about his report. "At least it won't be boring. Are you heading home?"

Daisy nodded. "I have verbs to conjugate for Latin class."

"Latin." He shuddered. "Miss Webster's too tough for me."

"I have English with her, too."

"Lucky you. I'm on my way to the firehouse. Why don't I walk with you?"

Tom Farrell was walking with her? Daisy warned herself not to read anything into it, but she felt her heart jump. She knew her cheeks had to be flushed, but she could blame the cold weather. She wore a secondhand tweed wool coat from a cousin over a dress she'd sewn herself, with kneesocks and lace-up shoes. She'd knitted her hat herself but hadn't worn mittens. Tom had on old clothes, hand-me-downs, no doubt, from his older brother. Angus Farrell had been killed in Holland last year. That was all Daisy knew. It was something no one talked about. She remembered him, always laughing, always with a good word for everyone. He'd been a medic in the army, and it was hard to believe he wouldn't be coming home to Knights Bridge.

Her father was out front when she and Tom arrived at the house. For a moment, Daisy thought her father might have relented about decorating, but then she saw he was sweeping the porch steps, grumbling about the postman's muddy feet. Unexpected guests were worse, even, than postmen with muddy boots. She was afraid he was about to lash out at both her and Tom, but Tom quickly stepped forward with a disarming smile. "Good to see you, Mr. Blanchard."

"Tom."

"I think we're due for a big snowstorm, don't you?"

"Could be. We'll know when it happens."

For a moment, Daisy thought her father might smile, but he didn't, just resumed his sweeping. Embarrassed, she turned to Tom. "Good luck with your book report."

"Good luck with your Latin verbs."

"Maybe I'll check out *A Christmas Carol* when you're

finished with it. It's an inspiring story. A cheap, grouchy man learns not to give in to despair and bitterness."

Tom eyed her, then her father, who didn't look up from his sweeping. More heat poured into her cheeks, this time because she'd been caught. She could see in Tom's expression he knew why she'd made her comment.

"I'll see you around, Daisy," he said amiably.

She watched him as he ambled across South Main to the common and made his way to the fire station. When she turned around again, her father had gone inside, shutting the front door behind him. He hadn't said a word or made a sound.

How much time were they supposed to give him? He simply wasn't the same man who'd left Knights Bridge in 1942. He and her mother had moved to town just before Daisy was born, scraping enough money together to buy the old house on the common. Married as teenagers, they'd been forced to leave their home in the Swift River Valley town of Greenwich, wiped off the map to make way for Quabbin Reservoir.

When her father left for the war after Pearl Harbor, the dams blocking the Swift River and Beaver Brook were doing their work, allowing the valley—stripped bare of everything from houses and businesses to trees and graves—to fill with drinking water for Boston to the east. When he returned in September, the seven-year process of filling the reservoir was almost complete. The town his family had called home for generations was gone, underwater. Hills he'd once sledded down were now islands.

Sometimes Daisy wondered if her father must feel as if he was back home in the valley, drowning under all that water.

She mounted the steps to the porch, neatly swept and barren of Christmas decorations. What would he do if she made a wreath and hung it on the front door? What would her mother do? But Daisy knew she wouldn't find out. She would respect her mother's wishes and give her father time.

As she opened the bare front door, she looked back at the common, Tom now out of sight. She was a more dedicated student than he was, but it wasn't just that. Homework gave her an excuse to stay in her room, away from her Scrooge of a father.

Two days later, Tom arrived at the Blanchard house with ice skates, the laces tied together, slung over one shoulder and a small metal box in his hands. Daisy had answered the doorbell, but her father was right behind her. She was caught off guard and didn't know what to say. "Did you finish your report?" she finally asked.

Tom grinned. "With minutes to spare. How did you do with your Latin verbs?"

"They're not due until tomorrow."

"But you're done, right? Good for you. I'm meeting friends on Echo Lake to go skating." His expression changed as he made eye contact with her father. Confident Tom Farrell suddenly looked uncertain and awkward. "Sir… Mr. Blanchard…" Tom cleared his throat. "I'd like to ask you a favor."

Daisy felt her father stiffen as he eased in next to her in the doorway. "A favor?" He grunted, clearly skeptical. "What kind of favor?"

Tom hesitated, then opened the box. Inside was a white candle, or what was left of it. Its wick was blackened, and melted wax had congealed on the sides, reducing it to a misshapen mass. Daisy saw that her father was frowning at it, too.

Either Tom didn't notice their expressions or was simply undeterred. He held the box toward her father. "I wonder if you would place this candle in your front window and light it on Christmas Eve."

"Why?" her father asked.

"For my brother."

Daisy gasped but her father remained still and silent.

"My mother made the candle when Angus joined the army. She promised to burn it every Christmas until he came home. Well…" Tom took in an audible breath. "He's not coming home, even to bury. Mom can't bear to burn the candle herself, but she said it would be all right if someone in the village did."

"Tom," Daisy's father said, his voice strangled. "Son…"

"I'll understand if it's too much to ask—"

"It's not too much." He put out a calloused hand and took the box. "We'd be honored, wouldn't we, Daisy?"

She nodded and managed to mumble a yes.

Tom smiled, tears shining in his hazel eyes. "Thank you."

With tears in her own eyes, Daisy watched the rugged, easygoing teenager cross South Main to the common, picking up his pace as he waved and called cheerfully to his friends.

It was at that moment she fell in love with Tom Farrell.

ONE

→←

"He told me, coming home, that he hoped
the people saw him in the church, because
he was a cripple, and it might be pleasant to
them to remember on Christmas Day who made
lame beggars walk and blind men see."

–CHARLES DICKENS, *A CHRISTMAS CAROL*

CLARE MORGAN HADN'T FELT THIS HAPPY in a long time. A *very* long time, she thought as she gathered up books to take to Rivendell, the local assisted-living facility. She prided herself on her self-sufficiency and independence—her professionalism as a librarian—and she was happy in countless ways, but this was different. This was happiness born of contentment. The uncertainties of the past few months were lifting and confidence settling in that she'd made the right decision to leave Boston and come to out-of-the-way Knights Bridge, Massachusetts.

New to the town and its small, charming library, Clare was getting a feel for the reading preferences of the seniors at Rivendell. Audrey Frost liked cozy mysteries, particularly ones set in England. Grace Webster would read anything but was partial to literary fiction and classic adventure novels. Arthur Potter had asked Clare to bring him all the Harry Potter books, since he and Harry shared the same last name and he'd always wanted to be a wizard. Daisy Farrell, Rivendell's newest resident, had requested *A Christmas Carol*, the classic Dickens story apparently a favorite with her and her late husband.

Almost everyone at the facility was widowed, but Clare gathered that many had enjoyed long marriages.

Except one feisty woman in her late eighties whose name Clare had forgotten. "I've never lived alone until four years, three months and eighteen days ago," she'd said when Clare had delivered her a stack of biographies. "It's heaven on earth."

Clare was a widow herself, but she wasn't sure how many people in her new town were aware that she'd been married. She had enjoyed the entire one year, two months and three days of her marriage to Stephen Morgan. Every single second had been bliss—including the inevitable arguments. That he'd been gone for six years seemed inconceivable. But every day she saw him in Owen, their six-year-old son, born seven weeks after his father's untimely death in a car accident.

She put the books in a box, careful not to overfill it and make it impossible to carry. The seniors also had several book clubs that met both at Rivendell and at the library. Vera Galeski, a part-time worker at the library, had taken Clare through the various book clubs. Her predecessor as library director, Phoebe O'Dunn, born and raised in Knights Bridge, had run a tight ship. She'd left Clare with a balanced budget and a well-trained group of volunteers, among them several mobile residents of the assisted-living facility.

She checked her watch. Three o'clock. Owen, a first-grader, would be walking from school soon to play with Aidan and Tyler Sloan at their house. So far, Owen was adjusting well to his new school. It had only been six weeks since his and Clare's arrival in Knights Bridge, and she expected bumps in the road—but small ones, especially compared to the huge one of losing Stephen. Owen, of course, didn't remember his father. He was a photo in an album, part of funny stories Clare told about life before he was born.

Stephen had been the love of her life. It wasn't something she told her young son, but she didn't hide it, either.

She got on with her work. She went out the heavy front door and took the ramp instead of the stairs. In anticipation of the run out to Rivendell, she'd parked on South Main in front of the library, a sturdy mostly brick building donated to the town in 1872 by George Sanderson, whose stern portrait hung above the fireplace in the main sitting room. As far as Clare knew, there were no Sandersons left in Knights Bridge.

She hit the button on her key fob to unlock the car doors. She popped the trunk, setting the box inside next to ice skates she'd found at a secondhand sports store in Amherst, a nearby college town. Owen desperately wanted to learn to ice skate. He insisted six was old enough. Every winter for the past fifty-plus years, the town had created an outdoor rink on the common. It was an "at your own risk" operation, with no supervision, no walls to grab hold of—not even a proper place to warm up. Hypothermia and frostbite were real concerns in a New England winter.

Clare put the brakes on her litany of concerns. *Questions*, she told herself. Not worries. She wasn't a panicky, overprotective mother and didn't want to become one. She was asking appropriate questions and taking appropriate precautions without turning either Owen or herself into chronic fretters.

But she'd been on South Main last week when two teenage boys had collided, requiring Band-Aids and a lot of cursing if not a trip to the ER and stitches.

Still…

Clare got in her car. Bringing books to the seniors at Rivendell was one of the easy, low-tech, low-stress parts of her job, and she loved it.

She glanced back at the library. It was decked out with twin wreaths on the front door, swags of greenery around the windows and a trio of grapevine reindeer next to the steps. Tasteful and festive. Decorating for the holidays was a long-standing tradition in Knights Bridge. According to the trustees of the Knights Bridge Free Public Library, most of the decorations, accumulated over decades, had succumbed to a roof leak last winter, but many had been in need of discarding or replacing. Few were missed. The library had its secrets, but not many treasures. By the time Clare started work, volunteers had already dived in to create new decorations, particularly with natural materials. Except for one anemic-looking grapevine reindeer, the results were impressive, and she and Owen had plans to rehabilitate the reindeer.

She turned off South Main at the end of the oblong-shaped common onto the main road out to the highway. Freshly fallen snow added to the festive atmosphere. What could be more perfect than Christmas in her small New England town?

This would be her and Owen's best Christmas ever, Clare thought, smiling as she drove on the winding road.

Knights Bridge's only assisted-living facility was located in a beautiful spot with views of snow-covered meadows that gave way to woods. In the distance, Clare could see a sliver of water, not yet frozen over, that she knew to be part of Quabbin, a vast reservoir built in the 1930s by the damming of the Swift River. Many of the elderly residents of Rivendell knew people who'd lived in the valley, or had lived there themselves, before its four small towns had been taken over by the state and disincorporated, their entire populations forced to relocate.

The "accidental wilderness," Quabbin was called now, with its protected waters and watershed. On a previous visit to Rivendell, Grace Webster, a retired teacher and avid bird-watcher, had told Clare about the return of bald eagles to the valley.

She grabbed the box of books and headed inside, setting the box on a chest-high wall unit in the corridor. She waved to the receptionist, who was expecting the delivery, but the young woman was dealing with a man in expensive-looking dark brown cords and a canvas shirt, its sleeves rolled up to his elbows, as he visibly tried to control his impatience. "Her name is Daisy Farrell," he said. "She's your newest resident. She's in good health for a woman in her eighties, but I want to review her care with your medical staff."

"Of course," the flustered receptionist said. "I'm sorry. I didn't realize today's moving day for Mrs. Farrell. I only just got in."

He calmed down. "Thank you."

One of those imperious, successful men who likes to get his way, Clare thought as she worked a sore muscle in her arm from carrying the heavy box. She would bet the man wasn't from Knights Bridge. Why was he interested in Daisy Farrell? Clare pushed her questions aside. It didn't matter. Whatever his reasons for being here, she doubted he'd ever show up again.

The man left the receptionist to fulfill his request and seemed to notice Clare for the first time. He glanced at the books in the box. "That's quite a range of titles."

"It's quite a range of people who live here." She didn't manage to keep the starch out of her voice.

If he noticed, he didn't pay any attention. "No doubt. Are you from the library?"

"Clare Morgan. I'm the new library director."

"Nice to meet you, Clare. I'm Logan Farrell. Daisy

Farrell—the woman I was biting off the poor receptionist's head over—is my grandmother." He breathed
deeply. "It's harder than I thought to move her in here."

Clare noticed a nick on his hand and bits of cardboard
on his shirt. She also noticed the muscles in his fore-
arms. He had short-cropped dark hair, hazel eyes and a
strong jaw—strong features in general, perhaps part of
the reason she'd misread him. She knew better than to
judge people, given her work and her natural disposition.
Logan Farrell might be impatient and even arrogant, but
he was here with his aging grandmother.

"She could use a cheerful book to read," he added.

Clare smiled. "I'm sure that can be arranged. She requested *A Christmas Carol*."

"I don't know how cheerful the ghost of Jacob Marley is. Scared the hell out of me as a kid. Have you met
my grandmother?"

"Not yet."

"She has a house on Knights Bridge common and used
to walk to the library, but she hasn't been out much since
she took a fall in November." Logan glanced at the nick
on his hand, as if noticing it for the first time. "I can in-
troduce you if you'd like."

Even if the offer was to assuage his guilt at getting
caught being impatient with the receptionist, Clare accepted. "I'd love to meet Mrs. Farrell," she said.

Daisy Farrell's grandson was clearly out of his element in a small-town assisted-living facility, talking to the local librarian. As Clare followed him down the hall, she wondered what kind of work he did and where he lived. Boston? Hartford? Somewhere farther afield—had he flown in to visit his widowed grandmother?

The door was open to a small apartment, where an elderly white-haired woman was standing on a chair, hammer in hand. She had on baggy yoga pants, a pink hoodie and silver sneakers.

Logan sucked in an audible breath. "Gran," he said. "What are you doing?"

"Hanging my sampler."

Clare noticed a cross-stitched sampler on a chest of drawers. Neatly stitched flowers and farm animals created a frame for the simple inscription:

The only way to have a friend is to be one.

Daisy Farrell in a nutshell, Clare suspected.

"I can hang the sampler for you, Gran." Logan put a hand out. "Come on."

She grinned at him. "Getting up here was easy. I figured I'd need help getting down."

"Had a plan, did you?"

"Enough of one. Let me finish and—"

"We have company," he said. "We can finish in a few minutes."

She sighed. "All right, all right."

He took her hammer and helped her down from the chair. "Gran, this is Clare Morgan, the new librarian in town. Clare, my grandmother, Daisy Farrell."

"A pleasure, Mrs. Farrell," Clare said.

"Same here," the older woman said politely. "You're not from town, are you?"

Clare shook her head. "My parents moved to Amherst after my sister and I went to college, but we grew up outside Boston. I lived in Boston until I relocated to Knights Bridge in November. My son's in first grade." She smiled. "We're both adjusting."

"Then you're married?" Daisy Farrell asked. "What's your husband do?"

"I'm widowed, Mrs. Farrell."

Clare noticed Logan's sharp look, as if he hadn't considered such a thing.

"Oh, dear," Daisy said, shaking her head. "You're so young. A fresh start here will be good for you. Knights Bridge is a wonderful town—not that I've known any other. Well, until now. I lived in the same house all my life. I was born in an upstairs bedroom."

Logan touched her elbow. "Here, have a seat, Gran. We'll get your sampler hung. It'll help this place feel more like home."

"It will, but I'm not feeling sorry for myself. You and

your father didn't drag me kicking and spitting into seeing I had to move. I knew it had to be done." She sank into a chair upholstered in a cheerful fabric. "Grace Webster says she'll let me borrow her binoculars until I get a pair, so I can watch the birds, and Audrey Frost wants to sign me up for yoga. What do you think of that, Logan? Audrey's younger than I am. Can I handle yoga?"

"I'll check with your internist, but I don't see why not, if it's designed for seniors."

"Well, I won't be doing headstands, I can tell you that."

"I just got you off a chair, Gran."

She waved a hand. "Life is full of perils."

Logan rolled his eyes, good-natured with his grandmother. "That's not an excuse for being reckless."

"Reckless." Daisy snorted and turned to Clare. "I fell doing the dishes. I've done the dishes every day for the past eighty years. Fortunately I didn't break anything when I fell. All's well that ends well." She leaned forward. "You can tell that to Dr. Farrell."

Dr. Farrell? Clare glanced at him and decided she wasn't surprised that he was a doctor.

"Dr. Farrell is glad you didn't break your hip," he said.

"I am, too. I'd have hated to have one of the Sloan brothers find me half-dead on the kitchen floor. I had them in to fix a leak in the cellar before winter set in."

Owen would be playing with the sons of one of the five Sloan brothers by now, Clare thought. Sloan & Sons was an established, respected construction firm in town. She hadn't figured out all their stories yet, but she did know that the sixth Sloan sibling was a woman and a main player in her family's company.

Clare nodded to the sampler. "It's lovely. Did you do the stitching yourself, Mrs. Farrell?"

"My mother did. I hung it in the kitchen where I could see it every morning." She sighed, staring at the simple stitches, then seemed to force herself out of her drifting thoughts. "Logan, don't you have more boxes to bring in from the car?"

"A couple more, Gran."

"I can help," Clare said without thinking, already moving into the hall.

"Thank you," Logan said, catching up with her.

His car, of course, was the expensive one parked next to hers. He opened the back door. "I have everything out of the trunk. I had a delivery service do most of the big stuff. Gran had everything set to go."

"She planned the move?"

"It was her idea." He lifted a cardboard box out of the backseat. "She said she wanted to make it easier on us by making the decision to move herself."

"That's sweet."

"That's my gran." He nodded to the box in his arms. "It's some linens she wants here with her. It's not heavy."

"I'll manage," Clare said, taking the box. "I'm used to hauling books."

He took a bigger, bulkier box from the backseat—clothes, he said—and they went back inside. "Let's hope she's not back up on that chair," he said as he and Clare came to his grandmother's apartment.

She was sitting in her chair, flipping through a small, obviously old photo album. "Here it is," she said, lifting out a faded black-and-white photograph. "This is the house decorated for the first Christmas after the end of the war. World War II," she added, as if Logan might not know. She handed the photograph to him. "I have one favor to ask, Logan. Can you decorate the house again, for one last Christmas before it's sold?"

"Gran…you know you don't have to sell the place."

"We'll talk about that later. You can decorate the house however you want, but if you look closely at the picture, you'll see a candle in the front window." She paused, touching the photograph. "Place a candle there, won't you? In that same window?"

"Of course," Logan said, clearly mystified by his grandmother's request.

"A real candle. Then light it on Christmas Eve, or get someone to light it."

He bent down and kissed her on the cheek. "I will, Gran, and we'll light it together on Christmas Eve. They do let you out of here, you know."

"You'll be in town for Christmas?"

He smiled. "I will now."

"But your work…" She frowned at him. "There are always a lot of accidents in Boston at Christmas. I don't want you to miss helping someone because you feel sorry for me."

"If I'm not at the hospital, Gran, another doctor will be. The emergency department has more than one qualified doctor."

"But you're their best," Daisy said.

Logan stood straight. "That's kind of you to say, Gran."

She shifted to Clare. "If I were in an accident, I would want Logan in the ER to stop the bleeding."

He changed the subject, asking her if she wanted him to unload the two boxes. Clare quickly set hers on a dresser. An ER. An accident. Winter…Christmas…

She noticed Logan narrowing his eyes on her with obvious concern and realized she was breathing rapidly. It was as if the exchange between him and his grandmother had transported her into her own past.

She'd had years of practice coping with such moments, and she pulled herself out of the spiral and forced herself to smile as she mumbled a goodbye and fled. As she got into her car, she told herself she could relax. She needn't be embarrassed or concerned she would have to explain her reaction. She'd known men like Logan Farrell when she'd lived in Boston, and she doubted she would run into him again. He'd get his grandmother settled, hire someone to decorate her house for Christmas and put her out of his mind once he was back in the city.

Vera Galeski, in her early sixties, was explaining to Clare the long-standing Knights Bridge tradition of singing carols in the village on Christmas Eve when Logan Farrell entered the library. Clare couldn't believe her eyes. He made no move to take off his black wool overcoat, a sign he didn't plan to stay long. He walked straight to her desk—again the brisk, efficient ER doctor more than the sensitive, loving grandson.

With raised eyebrows, Vera retreated to the children's room in the front of the library.

"I can't decorate Gran's house by myself," Logan said. "I get hives thinking about it."

He didn't look as if he were about to break out in anxiety-driven hives. Clare couldn't hide her amusement. "Really, Dr. Farrell?"

"Logan. Please. All right, hives is an exaggeration, but it's close. I don't want to disappoint my grandmother.

This move..." He paused, grimacing. "You help me decorate her house for Christmas, and the library can have first crack at her collection of books. Take what you want and I'll get rid of the rest. She's a pack rat. She could have valuable first editions."

"And your grandmother has agreed to this arrangement?"

"She proposed it."

Clare smiled. "Did you tell her about your hives?"

An unexpected smile played at the corners of his mouth. "She said, 'Logan, you look as if you're about to break out in hives.'" But he glanced at the library entrance, as if he was in a hurry and already had stayed longer than he'd meant to. He looked back at Clare, again the busy ER doctor. "You'll do it?"

The odds she would discover a hidden treasure buried in Daisy Farrell's house were slim to none, but the library did raise money from periodic book sales and could always use donations.

Logan shoved his hands in his overcoat pockets, an obvious attempt to hide his impatience. "I don't see a downside," he said.

You, Clare thought, but she tried to keep her reaction from entering itself into her expression. "I want to be sure I have the time. I'm still getting used to life in Knights Bridge, and I have a first-grader—"

"He can help. Kids love to decorate. I'll buy him a present. What does he like?"

She folded her arms across her chest. "You like to get your way, don't you?"

"I'm trying to help my grandmother."

"You're trying to fob off helping your grandmother onto me."

"I said I'd help."

"When?"

"I'm off this weekend."

Clare lowered her arms to her sides. "You don't have any plans to be in Knights Bridge on Christmas Eve, do you?"

"I don't have plans for Christmas right now. Clare—Mrs. Morgan—"

"Clare is fine, and of course I'll help decorate your grandmother's house—as a favor to her. She doesn't need to donate anything to the library."

"Not going to be bribed, are you?"

"I have a feeling you and Mrs. Farrell are both good at getting people to do what you want them to do."

"I'm an amateur compared to Gran." He sighed in obvious relief. "Thank you."

Clare expected him to bolt out of there now that he'd gotten his way, but he didn't move. He eyed her, his knowing gaze somehow reminding her he was an emergency physician. "Gran's mention of accidents at Christmas got to you," he said finally.

"I don't know why it did. I hope it didn't make her feel awkward."

"She's lived a long life. She's had her share of hardships and tragedies." Logan left it at that and stood straight. "We can start on Saturday, then?"

Clare nodded. "I have the weekend off."

"Good. It shouldn't take long to decorate the place. Let's meet at the house at nine. Will that suit you?"

"That works for me."

"Good. I'll see you then," he added, already on his way toward the front door.

When the door thudded shut behind him, Clare sank into the chair at her desk and breathed.

What had she just done?

Nothing dramatic or insane, she told herself. She'd agreed to help decorate a house with an intense, good-looking, out-of-town ER doctor who wanted to please his grandmother. Any romantic implications were in her head—not that she was thinking along those lines, or, certainly, that he was.

"Seriously," she told herself.

She was simply a means to an end for Logan Farrell.

It was dark when Clare left the library. She drove the short distance to Maggie and Brandon Sloan's fixer-upper "gingerbread house" off South Main. Maggie was a local caterer with enough energy for ten people. Putting bits and pieces of their conversations together, Clare had concluded that Maggie and her carpenter husband, childhood sweethearts, had come through a rough patch in their marriage.

Maggie had on a chef's apron covered in flour, some of it in her red curls. "It's pandemonium in here," she said cheerfully.

She wasn't exaggerating. Aidan, Tyler and Owen had transformed the living room into a pirate island.

"Brandon's brother is engaged to an actual pirate expert," Maggie said. "She's a good sport about the boys' idea of pirates. They just finished a treasure hunt, so your timing is perfect. All's well. No fights, no stitches." She didn't sound as if either would be out of the ordinary, or bother her, within reason.

Owen was flushed with excitement, enjoying his new friends. As he put on his jacket, he and the two Sloan boys made plans on their own for a future get-together, as if their mothers weren't standing there.

Maggie took the opportunity to lean in to Clare. "I heard you're helping decorate the Farrell house."

"News travels fast in this town."

"Audrey Frost told her granddaughter, Olivia, who told me, one of her best friends. Daisy's a peach. It'll be great to see her house decorated one last time. I can't imagine her not living there. I'm sure she'd love to have it stay in the family, but no interest there. It happens. People have their own lives."

"How many children does she have?"

"Just the son. Two grandchildren—a grandson and a granddaughter in Boston."

"I met Logan today," Clare said, keeping her voice neutral.

"That's what I hear. ER doctor in Boston. I'm surprised he helped Daisy move, but he's probably anxious to get her house on the market—not for the money, I don't mean that. Just to be done with it. I've run into him a few times when he's visited his grandparents. He strikes me as very efficient, the sort you want in an emergency if not for a heart-to-heart chat."

"Not strong on bedside manner?"

"You've met him," Maggie said knowingly. "What do you think?"

Clare considered a moment. "I think he's the sort of man who knows how to get what he wants."

"Daisy knows how to get what she wants, too. Trust me, if she hadn't wanted to make this move, she'd still be living around the corner. But I think her fall scared even her, and she hates to be a bother." Maggie peeled off her apron and tossed it onto the back of a chair. "If you need any help with decorating, you know where to find me."

Clare thanked her and left with Owen. She turned her attention to his day, but as they drove out to their small apartment in a converted nineteenth-century sawmill, she thought of the faded photograph of Daisy Farrell's house decorated for Christmas so long ago. For whatever reason, she'd latched onto the candle in the window. That, for sure, Clare thought, she and Logan could manage.

TWO

"Bah," said Scrooge, "Humbug."

–CHARLES DICKENS, *A CHRISTMAS CAROL*

LOGAN ARRIVED AT HIS APARTMENT IN A high-rise in Boston's Copley Square in time to get ready to meet friends for dinner. He pulled off his overcoat and headed into his bedroom. A quick change of clothes, and he'd be off to a hip, expensive restaurant. It wouldn't be a late night. He had to be at the hospital early. But as he pulled off his clothes, he felt dusty and tired, not from hauling boxes—from the emotions of the day.

Not like him, he thought.

He'd run the Boston Marathon. He'd survived the long hours and hard work to become a physician specializing in emergency medicine. Physical and mental fatigue he knew how to manage. Emotional fatigue…

He shook off the thought of it and forced himself not to give in to the mess of emotions that had been swirling around in his head since he'd arrived in Knights Bridge last night. He put on fresh clothes and headed out, walking over to Newbury Street and the trendy restaurant where his friends already had a table.

"How is sleepy Knights Bridge?" Paul, another ER doctor, asked when Logan joined him and his wife, Josie, a pediatrician.

Logan couldn't help but think of his grandmother spending her first night in her new apartment. Was she lonely? Disoriented? Immersing herself in memories of her home on the town common?

"Logan?" Paul shook his head. "*That* sleepy, huh? You're zoned out."

"Sorry. Long day."

"How's your grandmother?" Josie asked.

"Settling in. She's putting on a brave face, but it can't be easy moving into a new place after all this time."

"But she's thought about it," Paul said. "She's known this day could come."

"Not one for denial, you Farrells," Josie added with a smile.

"That's true. Gran's one of those people you think

will always be around. She's in her eighties, and I know better—I know there are more days behind her than ahead…" Logan didn't allow himself to go far down that road. "I like to think she's genuinely excited about her move into assisted living."

"It needed to be done," Paul said.

Josie rolled her eyes. "Mr. Sensitivity."

"What? It's true, isn't it, Logan?"

"We could have arranged for her to stay at home. She needs assistance. She knows that. She says moving into assisted living allows her to be independent and still get the help she needs at this season in her life."

"You sound like a brochure for the place," Paul said. "Martini?"

Logan smiled, pushing past his melancholy. "That sounds perfect."

But his mind drifted to Clare Morgan, the new Knights Bridge librarian, with her pale blond hair, blue eyes, freckles and shapely body beneath her winter layers. He'd observed a distinct back-and-forth in her between a spine of steel and a heart of gold. She'd pegged him straight off as an SOB. Not that he hadn't contributed to her opinion, but he suspected there was more to it than his impatient exchange with the receptionist—for which he'd apologized, again, before leaving his grandmother. The receptionist had taken his impatience in stride. He suspected she'd seen a lot in her work, but that didn't excuse his rudeness.

He tuned back in to the conversation with his friends. He ended up enjoying the evening—the martini, Paul's irreverence and Josie's sense of humor helped—but when he walked home, he noticed the festive lights and decorations celebrating the season and realized he hadn't paid attention until now. He'd yet to put up a tree in his apartment. He doubted he would bother. What was the point? He didn't entertain there, and he had no woman in his life. He remembered going out to the old Farrell farm on the outskirts of Knights Bridge as a boy with his grandfather. They'd go out into the fields and cut a Christmas tree. His own life had been in suburban Boston, not in Knights Bridge. He'd loved his grandfather, but when he'd died two years ago, Logan had realized how little he knew about Tom Farrell's life. His father had left Knights Bridge for college and life as a lawyer in the Boston suburbs. No one had been more surprised than Logan when his parents had decided to retire to the Farrell farm—just not right away. They were presently on a Christmas Market cruise in Europe.

Logan stood in his living room and looked out at the city lights. When his phone rang, he was surprised to see it was his father. "Is it snowing?" he asked when Logan picked up.

"Not at the moment."

"We have just enough snow here to keep things festive."

"It's six hours later there. What are you doing up?"

"I'm somewhere between East Coast and Austrian time. I'm sorry I wasn't there to help your grandmother move. I called at eight. She said she was about to tuck herself into bed. She seems content."

"I think so." They chatted for a few minutes about the move. Logan remembered the photograph his grandmother had pinpointed in the album. "Do you know if the Christmas of 1945 has any particular meaning for Gran?"

"It was the end of the war. Her father survived. He served in the Atlantic in the navy. He died when I was twelve, but he never talked about his war years—I'm not sure he would have with me, since I was just a kid. He and my grandmother lived with us. She died a couple of years after he did. The war..."

"A long time ago," Logan said.

"For us. For Mom, it must feel like the blink of an eye."

Logan stepped back from the window and its familiar view. "The local librarian is going to help me decorate the house."

"Good, because one thing we Farrell men have in

common—Pop, you and me—is not having an eye for decorating. You'll need the help."

"Do you ever wish you'd become a firefighter?"

"Many times. Pop was proud when I decided to go into the law—Mom, too. They said they understood I needed to be in Boston, but I'm sure they secretly wished I'd opened up a practice in Knights Bridge." He chuckled. "Well, in Mom's case, not so secretly, but she got over it."

"No regrets?"

His father was silent a moment. "Not when I see you and your sister, no. You've taken on a demanding career. The burnout rate for emergency physicians is pretty high. Take time to have a life, son. The work is good, but it will always be there. My pop used to tell me that. I wish I'd done a better job of listening."

Logan shifted the subject to his parents' cruise, but it was obvious his father was fading. After they disconnected, Logan took a shower, which he wouldn't have time for in the morning, his head swimming with memories. His grandfather's funeral, the church overflowing with well-wishers, Gran stoic but ever so sad. She was doing fine health wise, but given her advanced age, anything could happen anytime. She knew it, too. But she would tell him every day mattered, regardless of one's age.

By the time he collapsed into bed, he was happy that he had three twelve-hour shifts before his return to Knights Bridge.

Friday arrived faster than Logan had anticipated. He'd left clothes and toiletries at his grandmother's house and only stopped at his apartment long enough to grab a pair of winter boots. He didn't know why he'd need boots to visit his grandmother and decorate her house, but it seemed like a good idea to have them for a December weekend in Knights Bridge. He hadn't checked the forecast. For all he knew, they could be in for a blizzard.

The drive west was uneventful, with reasonable traffic and no snow or the dreaded "wintry mix." By the time he wound his way into Knights Bridge, the stars were out. Every house and business on the common was lit up for the holidays—except his grandmother's house. He didn't know why he hadn't noticed before that it wasn't decorated. He'd been preoccupied with the practicalities of her move, he supposed.

A few people—both adults and children—were skating on the rink on the south end of the common, their graceful and not-so-graceful moves silhouetted under portable lights. He'd gone skating with his grandfather a few times, never his parents or his grandmother. He couldn't remember the last time he and his old grandpa had hit the ice together, but Tom Farrell had skated until his last two years of life. Bundled up, Daisy would sit on a bench on the rink and watch him, her own skating days having ended in her early seventies.

"Eighty and out skating, Grandpa," Logan said aloud as he pulled into the driveway next to the house. "Not bad."

The house was as cold as a tomb—not the best image but it was in his head before he could stop it. Before he'd left town earlier in the week, he'd turned down the heat as far as he could without risking frozen pipes. Turning up the thermostat was the first order of business. While the heat kicked on, he unloaded the car.

A middle-aged man walked across the street from the common. "Hello, Logan. Randy Frost. I worked with your grandfather as a volunteer firefighter when he was chief. I just retired myself."

"It's good to see you, Randy," Logan said.

"Wasn't sure you'd remember me."

"Your mother is Audrey Frost. She's encouraging my grandmother to do yoga."

"She and Daisy are tight. Kind of the way it is here. In most small towns, I expect. Need any help getting Daisy settled?"

"I think I got most everything, thanks."

"Always feel free to ask for help. We'd all do anything for her."

The implication, however unintended, was that her own family had neglected her. Logan felt an urge to defend himself with the usual protestations about the demands of his profession, but Randy Frost wouldn't care and it was nineteen degrees out.

Randy didn't look as if he cared about the cold temperature, either.

Logan thanked him for his offer to help. "Were you ice-skating?"

"Me? No. I stopped by to watch Dylan McCaffrey skate with my daughter. They're getting married on Christmas Eve. He played professional hockey for a few years. Grew up in Los Angeles and ends up in the NHL. Go figure. You a hockey fan, Logan?"

"I'm a Bruins fan. I played hockey in high school but I was never any good at it."

"We can't be good at everything." Randy motioned toward the mostly dark house. "Daisy's got you decorating the place?"

Logan raised his eyebrows. "Your mother told you that, too?"

"She's her own Knights Bridge All News Network, but no, Clare Morgan mentioned it the other day."

"I see," Logan said, although he didn't.

"She lives in an apartment at the sawmill my wife and I run. It can be hard to be new in town, and everyone here loved her predecessor at the library, Phoebe O'Dunn. Phoebe's engaged to Dylan's business partner, Noah Kendrick. Southern California tech guy."

Logan smiled. "I'm lost."

Randy winked at him. "That's because you're not from around here. If you were, you'd follow right along. When do you plan to put the house on the market?"

"That's up to my grandmother."

"Right. Well, we know old houses around here. Let me know if you need to do any work on it before you put up the For Sale sign."

"I will."

Logan expected Randy Frost would turn around and walk back to the common, but he stood there. Scrutinizing the big-city doctor, Logan thought, feeling the older man's distrust. Logan understood Randy's wariness, shared by other people in town. To them, he was a busy physician from the city who hadn't visited his grandparents as much as he'd have liked—maybe as much as he should have. Obviously he hadn't visited as much as the people of Knights Bridge thought he should have.

"Good luck with decorating," the older man said finally, about-facing and heading back across the street before Logan could answer.

Relieved that little encounter was over, he went inside. The house was heating up nicely. He put away his groceries in a cupboard above the sink that his grandmother had cleared out for him before her move. "You're always welcome to stay here," she'd told him. "As long as I have this place, it's your home, too. You can toss out the rest of the stuff in these cabinets. I won't be needing it."

There'd been no self-pity in her tone, but that didn't mean other people in town didn't pity her—and blame Logan for her move into assisted living. His father, too. Logan understood that his grandmother could have decided to move and put on a positive face to spare her family, but he'd been looking for hints of doubt and hidden meaning and had seen none. She'd been adamant that whether to move was her decision to make, and she'd made it.

There wasn't any arguing with Daisy Farrell once she'd made up her mind, and if the rest of Knights Bridge thought he was a lout, then Logan figured so be it. He didn't owe them an explanation.

As he wandered through the first floor of the house, he noticed the places where the few possessions she'd taken to her new apartment had been. He could see her and his grandfather reading by the fireplace in the front room, watching the Red Sox in the family room, painting the woodwork in the hall. It was hard to imagine them apart, but after his grandfather's death, his grand-mother had taken Logan's hand into hers and warned him not to feel sorry for her. "I'm thankful for the years your grandpa and I had together," she'd said. "We were truly blessed."

More stiff-upper-lip nonsense, maybe, Logan thought with a hiss of impatience. How was he supposed to know if she was leveling with him? What had she done when he'd returned to Boston after his grandfather's funeral? Had she been at peace, filled with gratitude, on dark nights alone in this place?

But "alone" was relative, wasn't it? Knights Bridge, not just this house, was Daisy Farrell's home.

Or was that just a rationalization on his part?

Maybe he *was* a heartless SOB.

He smiled to himself, shaking off his melancholy. Time to get down to business. He texted Clare Morgan.

9 a.m. start still all right with you?

He tucked his phone into his jacket pocket and went out to the car for his boots. If he needed them, he wanted them warm. Shoving his feet into cold boots wasn't on the top of his list of fun things to do.

When he got back inside, Clare had responded. I'll be there. Can I bring anything?

He couldn't think of what. Glue? Fresh greens? A nail gun? Tape? He had no idea what was involved in decorating a village house for the holidays. He settled on a vague response. We can decide what we need when you get here.

Sounds good. See you then.

He didn't detect anything tentative in her response but wouldn't be surprised if she regretted agreeing to help. He supposed he'd taken advantage of her newness in town. It was natural for her to want to make a good impression. Helping decorate beloved Daisy Farrell's house would be a plus. But that hadn't been his intent. Logan wasn't quite sure how to describe his intent, but it probably had something to do with not wanting Clare to think he was a jerk who'd browbeaten a receptionist and forced his grandmother into assisted living.

Then there was Clare Morgan herself. He doubted she'd expected to run into anyone under seventy, except for staff, when she'd carried her box of books into the assisted-living facility. How could he have *not* noticed the curve of her hip and her unmistakable annoyance when she'd overheard him?

He noticed a library newsletter on a table by the fireplace. It included a note from the chairman of the board of trustees welcoming their new library director.

Logan sat on the couch and read.

Clare Morgan comes to Knights Bridge from the Boston Public Library, our nation's oldest public library. It's been her fondest dream to work in a small-town library, and with family roots in the lost towns of the Swift River Valley, she's pleased to be in our small town. Please take the time to welcome her and her son, Owen, to Knights Bridge.

"Well, well," Logan said aloud.

So, the fair-haired, book-toting small-town librarian knew something of the big city herself. He wondered how long it would take him to find out what had happened to her husband, then dismissed the thought. He could push people and rules to the limit when it suited him, but he wasn't crossing *that* line. If Clare wanted him to know, she could tell him.

Whatever her background, Logan figured he could do worse for decorating help. It could be Randy Frost showing up at nine o'clock tomorrow instead of pretty Clare Morgan.

Fruit, carrot sticks, cheese and a glass of wine sufficed for dinner. Soon after, Logan, bored, went upstairs to the back bedroom where he used to stay as a boy. It had been his father's room and he doubted it had changed since then. It had two twin beds with a matching dresser and bookshelves. He found a biography of Abraham Lincoln and crawled under the covers in one of the beds. He'd made it up when he'd stayed over earlier in the week. Until then, he'd never slept in this house alone. He remembered his grandfather chasing a bat that had swooped down the attic stairs, but that had been in the summer. Logan wouldn't have to deal with bats tonight.

Nightmares, maybe.

The pipes dinged and pinged with a rush of heat. Wind rattled the windows. A cat yowled in the backyard. Kids—teenagers, he thought—laughed and shouted at each other in the distance, presumably as the skating rink shut down for the night.

As an emergency physician, Logan had developed the skill for falling asleep anytime, anywhere, but he knew he had his work cut out for him tonight.

THREE

➤✦

"The happiness he gives is quite
as great as if it cost a fortune."

–Charles Dickens, *A Christmas Carol*

"WE NEED A BIGGER HOUSE, MOM," OWEN announced over breakfast. He was still in his pajamas, seated across from Clare at the small table that had come with their apartment.

"You have your own room," she said. She was still in her nightgown and bathrobe, enjoying the lazy winter morning.

Her son raised his gaze to her. "But you don't have a room."

"That's why there's a sofa bed. The living room turns into my bedroom."

He looked dubious. He pointed his cereal spoon at her. "*And* I can hear the brook at night."

"Even with the windows shut?"

"Uh-huh. It keeps me awake."

"Some people find water soothing. The brook will probably freeze before long, and you won't hear anything but the occasional trickle, if that."

"There are bears and foxes in the woods. Aidan and Tyler said so."

Probably true, Clare thought. "I saw three deer last night after you went to bed," she said.

Her son's face lit up. "Deer!"

"You'll see them soon, too. Now let's finish our breakfast and get dressed. We have a big day ahead of us."

He dug his spoon into his cereal. "I want to go ice-skating."

"I have something I need to do this morning. You can help me. Maybe we can go skating this afternoon."

"Aidan and Tyler said I could go with them and their dad."

"I want to be with you when you go out on this rink for the first time. It's not like the indoor rinks you know. Maybe we can go later."

"You said that last time."

"Did I? All right. We'll talk about it on the way into town. Hurry up."

There were times when Owen so reminded her of his father. Like now, she thought. He had the Morgan scowl, and somehow it made her notice his Morgan chin more, too. He finished his cereal, needed a reminder to take his bowl to the sink and then was off into the sole bedroom. Their apartment was charming and worked well for the two of them, but it *was* small—even compared to their apartment in the city.

But she loved the atmosphere of the renovated nineteenth-century sawmill, still with its original dam on a rambling, rock-strewn stream. Once she was settled in to her job and had a better feel for the town, she would buy a house in Knights Bridge. Right now, thinking about such a major change—planting real roots here—made her heart race. Her sawmill apartment was fine at least through the winter.

Owen came out of his bedroom chattering about ice-skating. There'd be no talking him out of it, Clare knew. The boy had the bit in his teeth and wouldn't let go. She had to find a way to make it happen that would satisfy him but reassure her. She hadn't told him about the secondhand skates yet. She couldn't place her finger on why skating made her nervous—perhaps because she couldn't skate worth a hoot herself.

Randy Frost greeted them as he walked down from Frost Millworks, located in a modern building above the original sawmill. The small mill provided high-quality custom millwork for construction and renovations throughout the Northeast, focusing on older buildings. Clare didn't know much about millwork, but she knew if anyone needed to duplicate a vintage window, this was the place to come. That had already happened with an 1830 Knights Bridge home during her short time in town.

"Louise has some extra greenery if you could use it for the library and Daisy's house," Randy said. "I've got it in the truck if you're interested."

Louise was Randy's wife, who ran the mill with him. "That would be great," Clare said, not sure how he'd found out about Daisy's house. "I'm on my way to town now."

"The good doctor will be there?"

She nodded without comment. Randy chatted with Owen as they walked up to the parking lot. He grabbed live evergreen boughs from the bed of the truck and put them into her trunk. Clare smiled. "They smell heavenly, don't they?"

That obviously hadn't occurred to him. She thanked him, and he wished her luck with the decorating. Once in the car, Owen immediately resumed pressing his case

for ice-skating. To add to the cards on his side, when
they arrived on South Main, Aidan and Tyler Sloan were
skipping up the sidewalk with their father, all three carrying ice skates. The boys eagerly invited Owen to join
them.

"I have a pair of skates for him in the trunk, but he's
never used them," Clare explained. "I haven't checked
them out yet."

But Logan Farrell came out of the house. "I can take
a look at them and make sure they're in decent shape.
What do you think, Clare? Would that be all right with
you?"

She nodded, trying to ignore the tightness in her
stomach as she popped the trunk to her car.

Brandon Sloan, a strong, competent-looking man,
eyed her as if he could tell what she was thinking. "I'll
stick close to Owen."

"He's only skated a few times and always indoors."

"Nothing like your first time skating outdoors. It's
not a lake or a pond. Even if the ice cracks, nothing
will happen."

"He's excited," Clare said. "It's easy to get ahead of
yourself when you're excited. He needs to pay attention
to the other skaters."

"I won't let him get bowled over," Brandon said, cuff-
ing Owen on the shoulder. "Right, kiddo?"

Owen giggled. "What's bowled over?"

"Flattened." Brandon grinned at Clare, matter-of-fact. "Helps to be clear with kids."

She appreciated his nonchalance but couldn't shake her concern. "There's also hypothermia—"

Logan eased in next to her. "It's not that cold today. He'll work up a head of steam."

"It'll be fine," Brandon added. "Relax, okay?"

Clare breathed, tried to smile. "Thank you."

Logan grabbed the skates and took Owen onto the porch to try them on and make sure they were okay.

Aidan and Tyler were clearly getting restless. "Two more minutes," their father told them, turning back to Clare. "Dylan McCaffrey will be out on the ice this morning. He was a professional hockey player. He's had stitches a few times, but he still has all his teeth."

"Hockey players wear helmets and play in indoor rinks with walls."

Brandon rested back on his heels. "You're getting yourself spooled up, aren't you, Clare?"

"I am. Sorry." She gave a small laugh. "Owen's had so much new to deal with—with the move. New home, new school, new friends. And six isn't five. He's getting more independent. I don't want to suffocate him but he's still so young."

"She's in mama-bear mode," Logan said, walking

down the porch steps with Owen trotting happily next to him, ice skates in hand.

"Got it," Brandon said with a grin.

"The skates are fine," Logan added.

Clare knelt in front of her son. "Now, Owen, you can go skating with your friends, but you have to listen to Brandon. Understand?"

"Yes, Mom."

"Aidan and Tyler have more experience skating than you do. That's okay. You don't have to keep up with them. You'll learn. Be patient with yourself."

Logan adjusted Owen's hat. "Best way to learn to skate better is to get out on the ice and go for it. Have fun."

Owen smiled up at him. "Thanks, Logan."

Already he was Logan, not Dr. Farrell? Clare kept her mouth shut as Brandon collected the three boys and headed across South Main to the common. She breathed deeply, her mind racing with possibilities of what could happen. Hurt feelings, the two more experienced boys running off and leaving Owen because he couldn't keep up, kids teasing him because he was the inexperienced skater—the new kid in town who didn't know anything.

Hypothermia. Stitches. Concussion. Broken bones.

"Clare."

She dragged herself out of her thoughts and gave another small laugh to cover for herself. "Mind wandering. Thank you for helping with the skates."

"Not a problem."

She remembered the boughs from the Frosts and returned to her trunk. "I don't know what we'll do with them, but they smell nice, don't they?"

"Sure do," Logan said, grabbing most of them.

She gathered the rest and followed him inside through the front door and down a center hall to a cozy kitchen with white-painted cabinets. They set the evergreens on the table.

He brushed off his arms. "I think I got spruce needles down my neck."

Clare laughed. "Me, too. At least we're not allergic. I mean—I assume you're not if you carried…"

"I'm not allergic."

She glanced around the kitchen, its cabinets and countertops worn but serviceable. The gas stove looked fairly new—within the past decade, anyway. Windows by the table and over the sink looked out on the backyard, covered in light snow. She imagined it in spring, with flowers, green grass and shade trees.

Logan stood next to her at a window. "Gran gave up keeping bird feeders. She had a bad fall hanging a feeder a few years ago. She doesn't give up easily, but she didn't want birds counting on her if she couldn't get out there in the snow."

"She'll enjoy the bird feeders at Rivendell, then."

"I'm sure she will. She'll have Grace Webster to instruct her."

"I understand that Grace is the Knights Bridge resident bird expert."

"That's what I hear." He nodded to the evergreens on the table. "Any plans for what to do with them?"

"I figure ideas will emerge as we get into the decorating. I assume we're only decorating outside. No point decorating inside if no one will be here."

"I did tell Gran I'd light a candle on Christmas Eve. I suppose I could delegate it, or drive straight back to Boston."

"Have you ever spent Christmas in Knights Bridge?"

"When my sister and I were kids. Grandpa would take us out on the tractor on the Farrell farm to cut a Christmas tree."

"You must have great memories."

"I'd give anything to cut a tree with him now. I don't care if I'm in my thirties."

"I gather from everything I've heard about him that your grandfather was something. I can see for myself your grandmother still is. Shall we get started?"

His eyes steadied on her. "What about your grand-parents, Clare?"

"All four are still with us. My paternal grandparents retired to South Carolina and love it, and my maternal grandparents live in Amherst with my parents. We have roots in the area. My family on my mother's side settled in Enfield early in the nineteenth century."

"One of the Quabbin towns."

"I always thought I'd be a small-town librarian, but I ended up in Boston."

"Because of your husband?"

"In part. I liked my job, too. And I like Boston."

Logan leaned against the counter, his arms crossed on his chest. "But it came time to leave and make a fresh start."

"Yes."

"Not just for Owen's sake—for your own, too?"

It didn't sound like a question. It sounded as if he al-ready knew the answer. Clare nodded. "Owen didn't need a fresh start. He was happy in Boston, but I thought the move would be good for both of us." She grabbed a pair of heavy-duty scissors out of a pottery container on the counter. "Why don't I trim some of the dead stuff off the evergreens while you check the front porch for a good spot for them?"

"Sounds like a plan."

His gaze lingered on her for a few more seconds. It was obvious he knew she'd deliberately changed the subject. She couldn't tell if he also knew he'd gone too far in asking about her reason for leaving Boston.

Did Logan Farrell ever worry about going too far with anything?

He headed down the hall without another word. Decorating his grandmother's house for Christmas couldn't be his idea of an exciting Saturday. He could have hired out the job, Clare thought, but he was here, doing it— if with her help.

She heard a screech and jumped, immediately thinking of Owen, but then realized it was a car hitting its brakes. But before she could relax she thought, *why?* Why was a car hitting its brakes hard on South Main? Had Owen slipped away from his friends to come find her?

She shook her head. "Stop. Just stop."

She realized Logan had come back down the hall and was standing in the doorway. "You all right?"

She smiled. "Just crazy."

"Ah. Crazy I can understand."

"I've been..." She snipped a browned twig off a bough. "I've been a little hyped up since we moved. Life's different here. We don't know a lot of people. Owen's making friends but I worry. A mother's prerogative, right?"

"Within reason," Logan said.

"A straight answer. I try not to let worrying get out of hand. I don't want Owen to be fearful because of me, or to decide not to do things because he doesn't want to upset me. It's a balancing act."

"He's moving from being a toddler under constant supervision to branching out a bit more."

"Owen's still under supervision."

"But he's six, not two."

"Or sixteen," Clare added with a smile. "I know what you're getting at. I had a dozen different scenarios flash before me as Owen went off with the Sloan boys."

"Did any of them end with happy, flushed faces and hot chocolate?"

She laughed, snipping another dead twig. "That's a perfect image."

"Gran's probably got cocoa in a cupboard."

"A plan for the day is developing."

"And," he said, entering the kitchen, "I found a good spot for your evergreens."

He grabbed a knife and helped Clare trim the boughs. Once finished, they took them out to the porch and arranged them on the rail, tacking them down with string he'd found in a kitchen drawer.

"Not bad," Logan said, appraising their initial handiwork. "It's a start."

"We can do more once we find out what all is available to us."

"Gran says she stores Christmas decorations in the attic. Are you game?"

Clare nodded. "Sure."

"You're not thinking about what could go wrong in the attic of an old house, are you?"

"Are you suggesting I catastrophize, Dr. Farrell?"

"Sorry. I was out of line."

"I guess you couldn't be an ER doctor if you worried too much about other people's feelings. You have to stay focused on what you're doing."

"It helps, but there's no excuse for being an inconsiderate idiot."

"Maybe, but I'd rather have a doctor with no bedside manner who's good at medicine than a doctor with great bedside manner who's not as good at medicine."

"You can have both in the same person."

"That's the best-case scenario, of course." Clare stopped herself before her mind could drift into the past. A Boston emergency department, rushing doctors and nurses and the worst news she could imagine. Aware of Logan's scrutiny, she pulled open the front door. "I love old attics. Shall we?"

"After you."

★ ★ ★

Logan led the way up to the second floor and then up steep, narrow stairs to a full attic under insulated eaves and heavy beams. Clare had expected an overstuffed jumble of dusty furniture and old trunks, but the attic, although jam-packed, was tidy, with cardboard and plastic boxes neatly stacked and labeled, two large trunks, four ladder-back chairs, a mahogany desk and several old bed frames.

Logan ran his fingers over the back of one of the chairs. "Grandpa was careful about fire hazards, and Gran's told us for years she's got the place in a 'dying condition.' Her words."

"Practical," Clare said. "She seems very organized."

He smiled. "That's Gran. Most of her books won't be up here."

"Logan, I don't need her books—"

"She wants you to have them." He squeezed between a stack of boxes. "She and my grandfather downsized their Christmas decorating once they hit their late seventies, and she did just the basics after he died. I doubt she's opened most of the boxes with decorations in ages."

Clare left him to search through the stacks of boxes and went to a window overlooking the common. She immediately picked out Owen on the ice, skating tentatively with Brandon Sloan. The rink was filling up, but the irrational surge of worry she'd experienced earlier had dissipated.

"Found them," Logan said. He stood in a dark corner, in front of boxes stacked to his shoulders. "Looks like there are four boxes. We won't need all of them."

"But it could be fun to go through them, don't you think? Maybe something will inspire our decorating."

His eyes lit up, maybe more than he would be willing to admit. He handed her the top box—obviously the smallest and lightest—but she insisted he add a second one. She headed downstairs, navigating the steep steps one-by-one, aware of Logan close behind her.

They set the boxes on the floor in the upstairs hall. He stood straight. "I don't have the attention span to dig through boxes and do all the decorating at once. What do you say we get this stuff into the kitchen and then take a walk?"

"Please don't feel obligated to entertain me. I can stay at this while you take a walk."

He grinned. "You don't mind a little tedium?"

"Define 'a little.'"

"Ha. Breaks are good. They keep you sharp, and we've been breathing attic dust. Time for some fresh air."

Clare wasn't accustomed to such a take-charge personality, but she didn't have to deal with him forever. Logan Farrell would be back in Boston and his life there soon enough. He'd make the occasional visit to his grand-mother and do his part to get her house sold as soon as possible. Clare didn't think her assessment of him was unkind and premature so much as realistic. He was a busy physician used to a faster pace than what Knights Bridge had to offer. An hour into their decorating proj-ect, and he was already bored.

"Just because I don't get bored easily doesn't mean I'm boring," she said, more to herself than to him. She wasn't even sure he'd heard her, but he paused, frowning at her. She waved a hand. "But that could be true for anyone."

"What does tolerating tedium have to do with being boring?" He seemed truly mystified. "Never mind. We can wait to take a break."

"I can tolerate tedium. That means I can go on for hours and hours without a break."

"I deserved that," he said, without any hint of re-morse. "I'm not going to leave you here to work by yourself while I wander off. That would seal my repu-tation in town."

"And your reputation would be—"

"Hotshot Boston doctor who neglects his grand-mother."

"So, not the best reputation."

He angled her a look. "You don't seem surprised or dismayed by my description of my reputation."

"Is it what you think your reputation is or what you know it is?"

"You tell me," he said.

"I'm new in town. I didn't know you existed until the other day."

"When you caught me being rude to a receptionist."

"I guess you can rest your case, then," Clare said with a smile.

"I *am* a jerk." He grabbed a box and leaned toward her. "But I don't neglect my grandmother."

Clare laughed, but she couldn't say whether he was half-serious or not serious at all. He trotted down the stairs with no apparent loss of energy after their trip to the attic. It wasn't that he couldn't go on for hours, she realized. He just didn't want to—not when it came to decorating an old house for Christmas versus handling medical emergencies.

She followed him down to the kitchen, where he set his box on the table. She put hers next to it. She peered at the contents of his open box, noting carefully packed gold, red and orange ornaments. Buried under a plastic bag of mostly broken ornaments—suitable for what, she didn't know—was a small tin box, intriguingly labeled *Christmas 1945*.

Clare lifted out the box and set it on the table. "The

label's not in the same handwriting as the other boxes," she said.

Logan took a quick look. "That's my grandfather's writing."

"It doesn't look as if it's been opened for years— maybe since 1945. What was special about that particular Christmas, do you know?"

"No idea. My grandparents were both still teenagers then." Logan didn't sound that interested. "Coat, hat, gloves and a walk?"

A here-and-now sort, Clare decided. She bundled up and joined him on the front porch. He wore a winter-weight leather jacket but hadn't bothered with a hat or gloves. He'd get cold, but he was a doctor—presumably he knew the signs of hypothermia and frostbite and would get warm before either took hold.

Then again, he could take her hand and get warm that way, which he did as they walked up South Main toward the library. "It's colder out than I thought," he said with a smile. "Your hand is nice and warm." He winked. "We can get little Knights Bridge talking."

"Blow any stereotypes of their new library director?"

"I imagine you've done that on your own already, without warming the hand of Daisy Farrell's city-doctor grandson." He eased his hand from hers. "I have my own stereotypes to fight."

"But you don't care, do you?"

He shrugged. "Not really. Sometimes I find myself fitting the stereotype of the rude, impatient, busy urban ER doctor. Do you find yourself fitting the stereotype of the introverted, nose-in-a-book, afraid-of-life librarian?"

"Is that what the stereotype is?" Clare smiled. "I do love to read. I like time to myself, but I have to deal with people all the time in my job. Afraid of life? Well, life happens whether or not we're afraid, doesn't it?"

"Is that how you ended up widowed?"

"In a way. In another way, I ended up widowed because death happened. Stephen, my husband, was in a solo car accident. He lost control of his car on black ice. A hundred different ways he could have walked away that night, but none of them happened. One of the couple of ways he could have died happened."

"He died at the scene?"

She shook her head. "No, he died in the hospital emergency room."

Logan was silent a moment. "I'm sorry. That must have been awful."

"It was. I didn't get to say goodbye before he died. I was working at the library, my last week on the job before staying home ahead of Owen's birth. I didn't get to the ER in time. But that's more than you need to know." She stopped on the sidewalk, looking across South Main at the snow-covered common, hearing the laughter and chatter of the ice-skaters. "I don't want to spoil your fun weekend in Knights Bridge."

"That's not possible."

She raised her eyebrows at him. "Trying to charm me, Dr. Farrell?"

"Is it working?"

"It might be." She glanced around them at the small-town winter scene. "Can you picture your grandparents walking hand in hand on South Main as a young couple?"

"I can," he said.

They went as far as the library before turning back. They carried down the rest of the Christmas boxes and opened one, discovering strings of indoor and outdoor lights—including a string of small outdoor white lights.

"They can't be more than ten years old," Logan said.

Clare lifted out a strand. "They're perfect for our evergreen boughs."

"Come on." He slung an arm casually over her shoulders. "Let's see what we can do."

FOUR

> "I have always thought of Christmas time...
> as a good time, a kind, forgiving, charitable,
> pleasant time...when men and women seem by
> one consent to open their shut-up hearts freely..."
>
> –CHARLES DICKENS, *A CHRISTMAS CAROL*

LOGAN AND CLARE BOTH WERE ALL THUMBS stringing the lights, but they got the job done by the time Owen and the Sloans returned. The four skaters, including Brandon, had pink cheeks and were at once sweating from exertion and shivering from the cold.

Owen proudly showed off a scraped wrist. "I only fell twice, Mom," he said, obviously pleased with himself.

"My mitten came off, but I got it back on before any-one skated on it."

Brandon cuffed him on the shoulder. "You're quick, Owen. Falling twice is good for the first time on a new rink and new skates. As far as I'm concerned, it's good anytime on skates."

"Dad fell," Aidan said, giggling.

Clare enjoyed the easy banter between the Sloan boys and their father. She took a closer look at Owen's wrist, trying not to embarrass him.

"He's fine," Brandon said. "There's no swelling. Good sign, right, Doc?"

"Nothing hot chocolate won't cure," Logan said. "Shall we make some? My grandmother has Dutch cocoa, and I bought fresh milk this morning."

Brandon had to get back to his house, but Clare vol-unteered to bring his two sons home after hot chocolate. They loved the idea, and Brandon agreed, reminding them to behave and be polite as he headed out.

Logan rummaged in the cupboards, unearthing a flowered teapot and ingredients for hot chocolate. The three boys wanted to know what was in the boxes on the table but didn't seem impressed when they peeked into the one that was opened and saw the collection of inexpensive ornaments.

"Don't tell Mom," Tyler Sloan said, "but I'm making her a snowman for our tree."

"That sounds great," Clare said.

Tyler nodded in agreement. "It is."

"Are you going to put up a tree?" Aidan asked, looking up at Logan.

"Here, you mean?" Logan shrugged. "I don't think so. I'm not sure I'll be in town for Christmas. Clare and I are decorating the outside of the house because my grandmother asked us to. I live in Boston."

"We used to live in Boston," Tyler said.

"Me, too," Owen said, yawning now that he was warming up. "I miss Boston. There are a lot of trees here. But I like trees."

"Can't go wrong with trees," Logan said.

But Aidan wasn't done yet. "Will you have a Christmas tree at your house in Boston?"

"It's an apartment, and I doubt I'll have a tree. There's a chance I'll be working on Christmas."

"Are you a carpenter like my dad?" Tyler asked.

Logan shook his head. "I'm a doctor."

"He'll stick you with a needle if you don't behave," Aidan whispered loudly to his brother.

"No needles today," Logan said with a smile, holding up the tin of Dutch cocoa. "Just hot chocolate."

The Sloan boys wanted marshmallows with their hot

chocolate. There were none in the house that either Clare or Logan could find, but Logan got the boys to agree to whipped cream with chocolate sprinkles. She didn't know how old the sprinkles in Daisy's cupboard were, but Logan didn't seem concerned. The cream was fresh, since he'd bought it himself for his coffee.

Soon, the kitchen smelled of chocolate and sweaty little boys.

With renewed energy, Aidan and Tyler donned their coats, hats and mittens and shot out the back door. Clare pulled on her coat to walk the boys back to their house. She assumed Owen would curl up somewhere with a book or beg her for her iPad, but he grabbed his coat, too.

"I could use some air myself," Logan said. "It must be ten years since I've had hot chocolate. It's making me sleepy."

All three boys ran out to the sidewalk. Clare resisted reminding Owen not to get too far ahead of her. He was past the age when he might dart out in front of a car—and there were no cars.

"Moving is one of life's big stressors," Logan said.

She pulled herself out of her thoughts. "Your grandmother seems to be adjusting well—"

"I'm not talking about Gran."

"Ah. I see. Owen's doing well. Knights Bridge is a big

change from what he's used to, but he likes it. He says so, anyway." Clare glanced sideways at Logan. "You haven't noticed anything off, have you? Sometimes it's hard to see when you're so close to a situation."

"He seems like a normal, healthy six-year-old to me. It's his mother I wonder about."

She couldn't hide her surprise. "Me?"

"Yes, you, Clare. You're jumpy. It's normal to keep watch over Owen. Not only is he adjusting to a move, but he's starting to be more independent. That can be tough on a mother, especially one in your circumstances."

"A single mother, you mean."

He shrugged without comment.

"Point taken." Clare smiled at him. "Making hot chocolate and decorating your grandmother's house for Christmas aren't what you're used to, either, are they?"

"Not even close."

"Are you restless away from the high adrenaline of your life and work in Boston, or is Knights Bridge a welcome break for you?"

"Am I climbing the walls, you mean?" He eased in closer to her. "Having the new town librarian to figure out helps."

"There's not that much to figure out," Clare said, ignoring a flutter in her stomach.

"We'll see."

They came to the Sloan house. Aidan and Tyler wanted to build a snowman and invited Owen to join them. Clare instinctively worried about her son overstaying his welcome, but Maggie and Brandon, joining their sons outside, encouraged her to let Owen stay. "I have four brothers and one pesky sister," Brandon said with a grin. "I'm used to a crowd. The more the merrier."

"I have your cell phone number," Maggie said. "I'll call when the boys have petered out. How's the decorating?"

"We've barely started," Clare said.

"I can only imagine what Daisy has collected after all these years. It's hard to picture anyone else living in the house." Maggie sighed, squinting against the bright sun. "Can't expect things to stay the same. I can remember Tom Farrell working on the skating rink. It was his idea to have one on the common. Hard to believe he's gone. He was such a presence in town."

But Aidan had lost a mitten in the snow and was blaming his brother, and Maggie was off. Clare started back to South Main with Logan. She noticed he'd said little. Maybe making hot chocolate had wrung all the small-town sociability out of him, but she suspected Maggie's talk of his grandparents had gotten to him, even if he didn't fully realize it.

"It's Gran's choice to sell the house," he said finally. "She doesn't have to for financial reasons. She's hoping someone else will have the desire and means to restore it."

"It's a beautiful place."

"It needs work."

"There are people in town who specialize in working on old houses. The Sloans as carpenters, Mark Flanagan as an architect, the Frosts for any custom millwork. They can transform your grandparents' house for its next century on Knights Bridge common."

Logan shoved his hands in his jacket pockets. "Maggie's right. It's hard to imagine anyone else living there."

"Maybe that's one reason your grandmother moved out," Clare said. "To help people start imagining someone else living there."

Logan glanced at her. "You can be wise when you're not jumping out of your skin, worrying your son might fall on the ice."

"Thank you. I think. Am I that obviously a worrywart mother?"

"Yes."

"You could have hesitated."

He grinned. "I know but I didn't."

They came to his grandmother's house. Even from the outside, it obviously needed work. New paint, loose floorboards on the porch repaired, shutters straightened, windowpanes replaced. She wouldn't be surprised if it needed a new roof. Inside—plumbing, electricity, heat, on top of cosmetic work.

It could all get expensive fast.

She smiled at Logan. "Our boughs look pretty good, don't you think?"

"Definitely." He slipped an arm around her. "Let's go see what's in that *Christmas 1945* box."

A candle.

An old, dusty, blackened, half-melted pillar candle.

It was the only item in the small box marked *Christmas 1945*.

"Well, that's anticlimactic," Logan said, plopping into a chair at the kitchen table.

Clare didn't disagree. "It looks homemade." She turned on the faucet, running hot water on the hot-chocolate dishes. "Do you think your grandmother made it herself?"

"If she did, it was the only candle she ever made in her life." He examined it without taking it out of the box. "A sorry-looking thing, isn't it? I suppose it could be Gran's work, but she was never that crafty. Cooking, organizing and volunteering, yes. Making things, not so much."

"Would she know how to make candles, given her age and upbringing?"

"No idea. It wouldn't surprise me if she does. This place was wired for electricity early on, so I doubt she grew up with candles. More likely she'd have used kerosene lamps, anyway."

"It could be a decorative candle, even if it's not that festive-looking to our eyes."

Logan touched a finger to the label. "The war had ended by Christmas of 1945."

"Was your grandfather in the war?"

Logan shook his head. "Too young. His older brother was killed in the war. I don't know much about him. My great-grandfather—Gran's father—was in the navy. I don't know much about his service, either."

"Do you remember him or did he die before you were born?"

"I never knew him."

"There's a lot of history in this house," Clare said softly.

He pushed back his chair and stood up. "The label could be misleading. Gran might have stuck the candle in the box without noticing the label."

"That doesn't sound like her. Look around here. Everything is in order. She might be a pack rat, but she's precise and very organized." Clare quickly switched off the faucet, realizing what she'd said. "I'm sorry, Logan. Of course you know your grandmother better than I do. I'm only starting to get to know the people in Knights Bridge."

"But you're observant," he said, clearly not offended. "If there aren't medical symptoms involved, I can be oblivious."

"Do you want to ask her about the candle?"

"I'll play it by ear. She's a strong woman who's seen a lot of life, but I'm not convinced she's not lying through her teeth about how ready she is for assisted living."

He tore open another box filled with decorations. Clare went through each of the boxes, picking and choosing what would work for the exterior and meet with Daisy Farrell's approval. Logan worked quickly, efficiently, not lingering on anything that looked, at least to Clare, as if it might call up memories. Either he wasn't one for nostalgia or wasn't opening himself up to letting it creep in. She suspected he wasn't one for it. He'd promised his grandmother he'd decorate her house for Christmas. Time to get the job done.

Clare discovered a pinecone wreath at the bottom of a box and decided she could refresh it. She cleaned the pinecones and added a red-ribbon bow and a faux cardinal she'd found in another box.

"I'm impressed," Logan said. "I thought for sure the pinecones were only good for mulch."

"If you don't look closely, you won't notice they've seen better days."

They took the wreath out to the porch and hung it on the front door, on a hook presumably there from previous Christmases.

"Window boxes," he said, pointing at the front windows. "I didn't think of it until now, but Gran used to decorate the window boxes for Christmas. Shall we give it a shot?"

"Sure, why not?"

She was aware of Logan eyeing her. "I suppose I should feed you first," he said. "You must be hungry."

"I can manage the window boxes."

"You can manage them better after a sandwich."

"Do you have sandwich fixings? We can always walk over to the country store and see what they have."

"I've already been to the store. We have ham, cheese, tomatoes, pickles, onion and a baguette. Does that suit you? Otherwise it's a can of soup from 1998."

Clare wasn't sure he was exaggerating about the date. "Suits me fine."

They returned to the kitchen, which still smelled faintly of chocolate. Her phone dinged with a text from Maggie Sloan: I'm feeding the boys.

Clare answered. Great, thanks.

She slipped her phone back in her jacket and relayed the message to Logan. "Maggie's a caterer, did you know? She did coffee hour for her book club at the library. She made an applesauce spice cake that I still dream about. I didn't resist."

Logan leaned in close to her. "Life can't always be about resisting."

He winked—sexily, provocatively—and set to making lunch.

Clare discovered a stack of about a half-dozen boxes in the dining room. The top one was marked Mysteries. She lifted it and set it on the floor, opening it up to books by Rex Stout, P. D. James, Dorothy Sayers and Ross McDonald. A first edition would be a find, but all of the books would be snapped up in a library sale.

"I read P. D. James with a dictionary next to me," Logan said, handing Clare a small baguette sandwich.

"She never underestimated her readers, did she?" Clare noted a paperback copy of *Fer-de-Lance*. "Nero Wolfe is a favorite with the seniors, and a teen book club just discovered him. He's timeless and yet part of another time."

Logan sat at the dining room table with his sandwich. "Did you become a librarian because you love to read?"

Clare sat across from him. "I'd love to read whether I'd become an accountant or a gardener."

"Gran told me to make sure I always had something

entertaining to read during medical school and my residency. It was good advice. I'd pull out a book on breaks and dive into another world, even if it was just for a few minutes. It was often hard to let myself believe I had the time, or that reading a paragraph of a thriller or biography here and there could make a difference."

"What kind of difference?"

"Perspective," he said, again without hesitation.

"To remind yourself that being a doctor doesn't mean you're all knowing? That kind of perspective?"

"That kind of perspective." His eyes held hers. "Also that there's life outside work."

She ignored another flutter in her stomach. "It's good just to get caught up in a story, isn't it?"

"I don't read as much as I'd like now." He smiled. "Gran wouldn't be pleased."

"Do you always take her advice?"

"I always listen to her advice."

"What advice didn't you take?"

"Get married before I turned thirty-two."

It wasn't the answer Clare had expected. "Why thirty-two?"

"It was a compromise between thirty and thirty-five. One was too young for what Gran calls the modern world and the other too old for her comfort. She was married at eighteen."

"You adore her," Clare said.

"Yes, and I'm hoping nothing in here makes me blush."

"Surely she's gotten rid of anything that might."

He leaned back in his chair, looking amused. "Are you implying my grandmother could have a secret life?"

"I'm not, but I am a librarian. I know that people are complicated."

"Ah-ha. What the doctor doesn't know about people, the librarian does."

She laughed. "I'll go along with that, but I doubt your grandmother has any secrets that would raise your eyebrows or mine."

"It takes a lot to raise my eyebrows."

Clare was on the front porch, fine-tuning the placement of the cardinal on the pinecone wreath, when Maggie Sloan delivered a tired, contented Owen. Logan, who'd brought out more strings of lights, opened the front door. "You can hang out in the front room," he told Owen. "We'll be in soon."

"The boys had a great time," Maggie said as Owen went inside. "We now have a family of snowmen in the yard to rival the family at the country store. The mother is wearing my best winter hat. *That* needs to change."

"There are loads of hats here," Logan said.

"If you can spare one that might not come back, that would be awesome. I can't guarantee a neighborhood dog or wandering wild turkey won't make off with it."

"The hazards of life as a snowman," Logan said, heading into the house.

Maggie appraised the decorations on the front porch, wisps of her red hair in her face as she turned to Clare. "You and Logan have worked miracles with this place already. Last year, Daisy barely managed a wreath."

"What about candles in the windows?"

"It wouldn't be Christmas in Knights Bridge without candles in the windows at the Farrell house."

"Do you know why?" Clare asked.

"I always assumed it's because Daisy liked them, but I don't really know. I doubt Tom cared one way or the other, so long as she was happy. Why?"

"Daisy asked Logan to light a candle on Christmas Eve."

"She and Tom switched to electric candles a long time ago. Maybe that's what she meant." Maggie sat on the porch rail next to the spruce boughs. "Tom would love that Logan is here."

"Was Tom pleased his grandson became a doctor?"

"I'm sure he was but I've never given it any thought. Logan's father left Knights Bridge for college and never came back here to live. No animosity—just life. He and his family would come to visit Daisy and Tom. Daisy and Tom would go visit them. Usual family stuff. I've always figured Logan got his grandfather's adrenaline-junkie gene. Instead of becoming a firefighter, he became an ER doctor." Maggie shrugged her slim shoulders. "That's my take, anyway."

"You must know everyone in Knights Bridge," Clare said.

"Not everyone." Maggie smiled. "But I know most everyone."

Clare glanced at the door, not wanting Logan to catch them gossiping about his family when he returned with the hat. But hadn't he just told her that life wasn't always about resisting? Even if he hadn't meant it—if he'd been flirting with her or teasing her to ease his boredom—it was a point well taken, something she often told herself when she let her *what if*s overwhelm her.

Such as what if he opened the door and caught her and Maggie talking about his family?

She became aware of Maggie frowning at her. "You okay, Clare?"

"Sorry. Lost in thought."

"Don't worry about talking about the Farrells." She grinned, good-natured and unrepentant. "We all talk about everybody around here. Part of being a good neighbor, right? Anyway, I need to run. I'm catering a get-together at the Farm at Carriage Hill tonight. Have you been out there yet?"

"I have. The house looks so charming. I didn't realize it was on a dead-end road. I turned around at the Quabbin gate and came back home."

"Next time stop in and say hi. I'll show you around if I'm there. Have you met Dylan and Olivia?"

Clare shook her head. "Not yet."

"To think that less than a year ago, none of us knew Dylan's father had bought Grace Webster's old house up the road from Olivia's place—never mind that she's his birth mother. A real tragedy that he died a short time later, but at least he got to meet Grace."

"I'm lost," Clare said. "Grace had a son?"

"It's one of the best stories ever around here," Maggie said. "But it's sad, too. Grace and a British flyer fell for each other just as she and her family were being forced out of their home in the valley to make way for Quabbin. He went back to England, never to return. He was killed early in the war."

Clare recalled hearing bits and pieces of the story but hadn't realized it involved elderly Grace Webster. "Now Dylan—Grace's grandson—is marrying a local woman, and they're building a house and a business together."

"Several businesses at the rate Dylan's going. He's not one to stand still. Olivia, either. She and I have dipped a toe into making goat's milk soaps. We use milk from my mother's goats." Maggie jumped down from the porch rail. "I should get rolling. That applesauce-spice cake isn't going to bake itself. You'll get up to speed on the goings-on in Knights Bridge. Just have to figure out how deep you want to dig."

"Deep enough to do my job," Clare said.

"And live here, too, I hope. You don't plan to buy a house in another town, do you?"

"No plans to do anything right now, but Owen is lobbying me for a bigger house."

"He says you sleep on the couch. Could do worse. When Brandon and I were in a rough patch last year, he slept in a tent." Maggie waved a hand before Clare could register her confusion. "Long story with a happy ending."

Logan came out onto the porch. "Perfect for a snowman," he said, handing Maggie a green plaid beret.

"Much better than my merino-wool hat. Thanks, Logan."

She trotted down the steps and out to South Main. Once she disappeared, Logan turned to Clare. "Owen fell asleep on the couch. What do you say we let him nap and open up a few more boxes?"

A Recipe for Applesauce Spice Cake with Maple Frosting or Cream Cheese Frosting

—— >‹ ——

CAKE

 2½ cups all-purpose flour or cake flour
 1 teaspoon salt
 ¼ teaspoon baking powder
 1½ teaspoons baking soda
 ¾ teaspoon cinnamon
 ½ teaspoon allspice
 ½ teaspoon cloves
 1¾ cups sugar (scant)
 1½ cups unsweetened applesauce
 ½ cup water
 ½ cup unsalted butter
 2 eggs
 ½ cup chopped walnuts (optional)
 ¾ cup raisins (optional)

1. Preheat oven to 350°F. Butter and flour two 8" or two 9" round cake pans or one 9"x13" pan.

2. Mix first 7 dry ingredients in medium bowl. Blend sugar, applesauce, butter, eggs and water in large bowl. Add dry ingredients and combine on low mixer speed just until blended. Turn mixer to high speed for about 3 minutes. Fold in optional walnuts and/or raisins by hand.

3. Pour batter into pans and bake. Plan on about 30–35 minutes for 9-inch layers and a bit longer for 8-inch layers; 50

to 60 minutes for a rectangular pan. A toothpick or tip of a sharp knife inserted into the center of the cake should come out clean.

4. When the cake is cool, frost with maple frosting or cream-cheese frosting.

MAPLE FROSTING

4 tablespoons butter (preferably unsalted)
¼ to ⅓ cup pure maple syrup
1 teaspoon pure vanilla extract
2½ cups confectioner's sugar
2 to 3 tablespoons milk (preferably whole)

Blend together butter, syrup, vanilla and about a third of the sugar. Alternate milk and sugar. Use as much milk as needed for consistency. If necessary, refrigerate cake before serving to set frosting.

CREAM CHEESE FROSTING

8 oz. cream cheese, softened (preferably full fat)
4 tablespoons unsalted butter, softened
2½ to 3 cups confectioner's sugar
1 teaspoon vanilla (or a bit more to taste)

Blend together cream cheese and butter with enough confectioner's sugar for good spreading consistency. Stir in vanilla. Refrigerate frosted cake before serving.

FIVE

Its dark brown curls were long and free;
free as its genial face, its sparkling eye,
its open hand, its cheery voice, its unconstrained
demeanour, and its joyful air...

–CHARLES DICKENS, *A CHRISTMAS CAROL*

CLARE MORGAN WAS UNDER HIS SKIN.

Logan acknowledged that fact with the clarity and
briskness he was accustomed to exercising in his work.
Knights Bridge wasn't a hospital emergency room, and
Clare wasn't a patient or the family member of a patient. But he couldn't dance around the reality in front
of him—staring him in the face.

He filled two water glasses at the sink. He and Clare

had checked the last of the stack of book boxes in the dining room, and she was back at the kitchen table, her fair hair out of its pins, her sweater askew, her face flushed. He noticed the curve of her hip, the shape of her breasts, the blue-green of her eyes...

It wasn't good, this attraction to the new town librarian.

Owen had awakened and was sorting through a small box containing a crèche Logan had forgotten his grandparents had owned. Clare and her six-year-old had already discussed the difference between a donkey and a mule. The wise men now had Owen's attention.

Logan knew he should leave the Morgans and run out to see his grandmother. They could find their way home. He would say thanks for the help and get back to his life. Staying here, letting his attraction take hold, was like hanging his toes off the edge of a cliff—tempting fate. He'd buried himself in work and now had a chance to have a good time with an attractive woman. Why play it safe?

Safe, however, was what Clare wanted and needed.

His grandmother would expect him not to cause trouble in her hometown. Help her get settled and decorate her house. Be nice to people. Then go home and come back to visit when he could. She had her full faculties and would see to selling the place.

If he gave in to the urge to kiss Clare Morgan he risked stirring up trouble.

Maybe that was why he wanted to do it. He was bored and restless, and he needed a distraction. If there wasn't a fire for him to put out, then he'd start one. His grandfather used to tell him that his own low tolerance for boredom was what had prompted him to become a firefighter. He didn't wish anything upon anyone, but he knew if the worst happened, he had the constitution to deal with it. *You remind me of myself at your age*, he'd told Logan. He'd figured out early on in his training that he was suited to emergency medicine.

He did what had to be done. People counted on him for that. It was his job.

It was *not* his job to mix it up with Clare Morgan.

His hard-driving personality worked well in his chosen profession. It worked less well in his personal life. He needed to behave himself in Knights Bridge. He wasn't going to have everyone in town peg him as a cad. His grandmother especially.

He wasn't going to *be* a cad.

Such a great word, he thought with a smile. *Cad.* To him a cad was a man who used a woman for his own needs, without regard to anything else. Here he was, decorating his grandparents' home for Christmas, a season to ask more, not less, of himself. He owed it to Daisy and Tom Farrell to hold himself to a higher standard.

And if Clare would rather he didn't? What if a bit of a cad would do her life good right now?

He shook off the thought and set the water glasses on the table for Clare and her son. "I'd like to check on my grandmother," he said. "I want to see if she needs me to bring anything else for her new apartment. Care to join me?"

Clare drank some water. He noticed her full mouth, the slender hands. Not helpful, but what could he do? If she noticed his reaction to her, she gave no sign of it as she set her glass on the table. "I'd love to join you."

"Is this the place with the old people?" Owen asked.

Logan smiled at the boy. "Yes, it is. Do you have grandparents, Owen?"

"I have *lots* of grandparents."

"My grandmother is learning about birds. We can have a look at the bird feeders she and her friends have set up for the winter."

"Aidan knows everything about raptors. They're birds of prey." Owen paused, very serious now. "They eat baby birds."

Clare looked slightly horrified, but Logan grinned. "I doubt we'll see any owls and hawks at the bird feeders, and no baby birds are up here this time of year."

The boy allowed that was likely the case. They grabbed their coats and agreed to Logan's suggestion they go in his car, Clare explaining she and Owen would have to come back to town, anyway, given where they lived. "We live in a *sawmill*," Owen said, climbing into Logan's backseat. "It's on a waterfall. It's cool but Mom has to sleep in the living room."

"It's not a problem," Clare said. "It's temporary—until we decide where we want to live."

"I want to live in Knights Bridge," Owen said, slightly panicked. "We're not moving again, are we? I have friends here."

"I meant where to live in Knights Bridge," Clare amended, pulling on her seat belt.

Owen relaxed. "Oh. Okay."

When they arrived at Rivendell, all was quiet. One of the dining room workers was outside, drinking coffee and checking her phone. She waved as Logan, Clare and Owen got out of the car. "Beautiful afternoon, isn't it?" she said with a smile. "Have to enjoy above-freezing temperatures when we have them."

Logan didn't have the heart to tell her the temperature had again dipped below freezing. Technically, it had gone above thirty-two degrees that afternoon but he doubted it had been for more than an hour. Winter was arriving in New England. The weather would get worse before it got better, but he had to admit he loved this time of year. Clare seemed content, bundled up against the cold. She unzipped her jacket as they went inside. Owen had refused to zip his jacket. Logan supposed he'd been oblivious to the cold at six, too.

They found his grandmother in the sunroom with her longtime friend Grace Webster, a retired schoolteacher in her nineties. Grace's grandson, Dylan McCaffrey, the only child of the baby boy she'd borne secretly in her late teens and allowed to be adopted, was funding an updated technology room and expanded gardens for the facility.

Frail but otherwise in good physical and mental health, Grace was pointing out where an intrepid, clever squirrel had gotten into one of the feeders outside the floor-to-ceiling windows. "We think it's only one squirrel," she said. "He's diabolical."

"Would a raptor eat him?" Owen asked.

Clare inhaled at her son's blunt question, but Grace motioned for him to come closer to her. She then launched into an explanation of squirrels and winter bird feeding, her decades of teaching in evidence. She commanded Owen's full attention, especially when she told him she'd seen bald eagles now that they'd returned to the area, given the protected Quabbin wilderness.

Using just her cane—no walker today—Daisy got to

her feet. "What a sweet boy," she said, addressing Clare. "How's he adjusting to Knights Bridge?"

"Very well, thanks," Clare said.

"My friends and I used to swim out at the old sawmill, before it was turned into an apartment. I still have the scar on my knee where I slipped on the rocks. I dived right back in, blood and all. Nowadays I suppose someone would have used their cell phone and called an ambulance."

"You probably could have used stitches," Logan said.

She waved a thin hand. "I've never had stitches in my life. Well, I suppose I did when I had my gallbladder out. But that's—what do the kids say now? TMI? Too much information? Or isn't that a current phrase anymore?" She didn't wait for a response, instead smiling at her grandson and taking his hand. "It's good to see you. How's the decorating?"

"It's almost done. Clare's been helping."

"Oh, good. Decorating needs a woman's touch, especially if a Farrell man is involved."

Randy Frost entered the sunroom with his mother, Audrey, another of Daisy's friends. They joined Grace's bird discussion. Owen was clearly enthralled, and Randy offered to look after him while Clare and Logan went with his grandmother back to her apartment. Randy gave Logan what he could only describe as a suspicious look—it was more than appraising or neutral but a notch below hostile. The sort of look that forced Logan to consider his reputation in Knights Bridge.

Then again, maybe Randy had simply detected Logan's war with himself over his attraction to Clare. Since she was renting an apartment from the Frosts, the older man would naturally feel protective of her. Logan didn't know Randy Frost well. It was possible he often looked suspicious.

Logan knew better than to offer his grandmother help as they walked down the hall to her apartment. Not only didn't she want his help, it was good for her to manage on her own. One of the attractions of assisted living, she'd told him, was being able to see people and do things she couldn't do at home—like chat about birds and go to yoga class with her friends.

"A pair of cardinals stay here all winter," she said. "I haven't spotted them yet. The bright red of the male will be something to see against the white snow. I hated giving up my bird feeders at home."

"You had plenty to do," Logan said.

"That's true. I've never been bored—not even since Tom died. Lonesome, but that's different."

She pointed out apartments of people she knew. Most of the doors were decorated for the season with indoor wreaths, Santa Clauses and tiny reindeer and sleighs.

Logan noticed his grandmother's door was bare and saw that Clare noticed, too. "Would you like us to bring you some decorations from your house?" she asked once they were inside the small apartment.

"That would be lovely," Daisy said, easing onto her chair. She put her cane aside. "I don't need anything elaborate. Just a little something to remind me it's Christmas."

"Owen collected the pieces to a crèche we found," Clare said.

"That would be perfect. We got that when Logan's father was a little boy. I'd love to have it here."

"And something for the door," Clare added. "A small indoor wreath made of some of your Christmas decorations? I think we could pull that off."

"I'd love it."

"I'll see to it," Logan said.

"The office has a list of restrictions. It's what you'd expect in a building full of senior citizens. Common sense." Daisy smiled and leaned toward Clare, a conspiratorial glint in her aged eyes. "They don't want us having anything highly flammable."

Logan smiled. "As you say, common sense."

"Speaking of flammable," Clare said. "We found a small box labeled *Christmas 1945*. Its only contents is a candle. It looks homemade. I was wondering—"

"A candle?"

Logan eyed his grandmother with concern. Her breathing was rapid and shallow, and she clutched her shirt at her chest as she stared up at Clare.

Clare went still. "I'm sorry. I don't mean to upset you."

But Logan could see that his grandmother wasn't hearing her. She was lost in her own thoughts—something triggered by the mention of the candle. "A candle," she repeated. "Yes... I... I..."

"Gran." Logan spoke sharply but gently. He knelt on one knee in front of her and took her hand. "Gran, it's okay. Breathe normally."

She gulped in air, fast, clearly hyperventilating.

"What can I do to help?" Clare asked.

"Nothing. She's fine." He took his grandmother's hand, checking her pulse. "Gran, hold your breath for a second or I'm going to throw a paper bag over your head."

She nodded, shutting her eyes, calming herself. Her breathing returned to normal. She squeezed Logan's hand. "I'm all right."

Clare stood next to him, shivering. "I'm sorry," she mumbled. "I'm so sorry."

Before he could reassure her, she about-faced and fled from the apartment.

"Oh, dear," his grandmother said, already stronger. "Now look what I've done."

"You didn't do anything, Gran."

"You'll see to her?"

"Once I know you're not going to pass out on the floor."

"Would it be okay if I pass out in my chair? Honestly, Logan, has anyone ever talked to you about your bedside manner?"

He grinned. "Often."

"You remind me of your grandfather," she said, sinking back into her chair. "It was a bit of a shock, that's all. That candle…" She closed her eyes. "Go see to Clare."

"I'll be back in a few minutes," Logan said.

"Take your time. I'm not going anywhere."

Logan found Clare on a patio outside the front entrance, pacing, clearly upset. "My grandmother is fine," he said. "She hyperventilated, that's all. It could happen to any of us."

"But at her age—"

"It looks worse at her age. Everything does. She gripes about it all the time. At Thanksgiving she told me that if she gets a piece of popcorn stuck in her teeth people panic, thinking she's about to keel over."

"She is very elderly, Logan."

"Yes, she is. It can be tricky to balance her desire for independence with her legitimate geriatric needs. That's one reason this place will be so good for her. That might not be the case for every senior, but it is for her—by her own account. And I believe her."

Clare shivered, her jacket open against the cold air. "It's my fault she got upset. I should never have asked her about the candle. I get curious and then I start asking questions that I have no business asking."

"That's part of what makes you a good librarian. If you hadn't mentioned the candle, I would have. It was an innocent mistake, if it even was a mistake. Don't be so hard on yourself."

"If she'd had a heart attack—"

"She didn't," Logan said, trying to break through Clare's self-recriminations. "And if she had, it still wouldn't be your fault."

She squeezed her eyes shut and nodded. "Sorry." She breathed deeply, then exhaled slowly, obviously a practiced move. She opened her eyes again and smiled at him. "I'm not as accustomed to medical emergencies as you are."

He decided not to tell her that his grandmother hadn't experienced a medical emergency. It obviously had looked worse to Clare. He touched her shoulder. "Okay now?"

She nodded. "Nobody likes to scare the hell out of an old lady."

He laughed at her unexpected irreverent humor. "Gran would agree. She feels terrible she upset you."

"It's not her fault!"

"See how that works?"

"Point taken," Clare said, calmer. "I should see about Owen."

"They won't let him run off, but Randy Frost might hunt you down."

"I noticed he looked daggers at you. Do you two have a history?"

Logan pulled open the door, letting Clare walk in ahead of him. "Not one that I know of. He's protective of you, isn't he?"

"He looks out for Owen and me. I don't know if I'd call it protective. But what's that got to do with the look he gave you?"

"Mmm. What, indeed?"

Her cheeks flushed red, and Logan grinned, realizing she had just figured out *what, indeed?* Had she been oblivious to his attraction to her until now? She shot ahead of him back inside, but she hesitated when she reached his grandmother's apartment.

He eased past her and went in first. His grandmother

was dozing in her chair. "I'll let her sleep," he said. "I can come back later."

Clare stood next to him. "My grandmothers are both in their eighties. They're such a presence in my life. You want to think they're going to be there forever..." She trailed off. "We're lucky to have them with us."

He leaned in close to her. "Now I really do want to kiss you," he said in a low voice.

She blinked at him. "What?"

"Imagine the ruckus if I kiss you and Gran wakes up or Randy Frost walks in here. Not to mention Grace Webster. She's been retired for thirty years, but I bet she can still rap knuckles with her ruler."

"Do you think she ever rapped knuckles?"

Logan grinned. "No doubt in my mind."

He kissed Clare lightly on the top of her head—sort of like a friend, except not really. He could smell her hair, feel its softness. She entwined her fingers with his, just for a second, long enough to tell him that she didn't object.

"We should go before we start a scandal," she whispered.

Would that be such a bad thing? Logan thought, amused. He walked over to his grandmother and kissed her on the forehead. "See you soon."

"Good," she said without opening her eyes.

"Didn't realize you were awake."

"And you a doctor."

But she was barely awake—just awake enough to let him know she was aware of the exchange between him and Clare. He might have been embarrassed if he thought his grandmother realized what he'd been thinking. Then again, she hadn't lived eighty-plus years alone on Mars. She knew the score.

Clare went out ahead of him. When he met her in the hall, she let out a breath and raked a hand through her pale hair. "You keep it up, Logan, and I'm not going to be able to live in this town. There will be rumors about us all over this place by nightfall. They won't stay within these walls, either."

"Rumors? I did just kiss you, and you did just willingly grab my hand."

"I didn't *grab* your hand. I…" She fumbled for the right word. "I got caught up in the moment."

"My point."

She sighed, a smile playing at the corners of her mouth. "I'm going to be smart this time and not respond."

When they reached the sunroom, Owen was outside at the bird feeders with Randy Frost. Grace Webster was reading, and Audrey Frost was crocheting. "I can only look at birds and snow for so long without doing something," she said.

Randy popped his head in the door. "Why don't I take Owen back to the mill with me? He wants to ride in my truck. Let you two finish decorating."

"Your truck?" Clare grimaced. "Is it safe for a six-year-old?"

"I was a volunteer firefighter for thirty years. We'll be okay."

She smiled. "Of course you will. Thank you."

Owen waved to her at the window. Randy chuckled. "He's been pressing up against the glass and making faces at my mother. We'll know what fingerprints are his. He's the only kid here." Randy seemed to enjoy having Owen to entertain. He turned back to Clare. "We'll plan on giving him dinner at the house if you run late."

Logan didn't detect any animosity in Randy's tone, just a knowing look as Logan left with Clare. He had no inclination to disabuse Randy of his suspicions. He wouldn't be surprised if most of them were true, anyway.

Clare was quiet as they left the facility and went back outside and got into his car. "What's on your mind, Clare Morgan?" Logan asked as he eased behind the wheel.

"Nothing."

"Usually someone as quiet as you are right now has more than nothing on her mind."

"Owen…" She glanced back at the building where she'd left her son. "First skating with the Sloans, then lunch with them—then a nap because he was so worn out. Now off with Randy Frost."

"And?"

"Owen won't think I'm neglecting him, will he?"

"He'll think you've moved to a great little town."

"It's been just the two of us for so long..." She smiled at him as he started the car. "I sometimes come up to the line of being an anxiety-driven and overprotective mother, especially since our move, but I don't often cross it."

"Depends where you draw the line. It's easy to label people."

"Do people label you?"

"I hope so."

She laughed. "You're not serious."

"What kind of label would I have?"

"Hard-driving, sexy ER doctor?"

"That's not bad. I could live with that."

"Hard-driving, sexy ER doctor who leaves a trail of broken hearts behind him?"

He backed out of the parking space, very aware of her next to him. "I guess you could just add narcissistic cad of an ER doctor to the label."

"Then you're not denying it," she said.

"I'm hard-driving, and I'm an emergency physician.

I'm not denying that." He shifted out of reverse into first gear. "It's for others to decide if I'm sexy or a cad."

"Or both. A trail of broken hearts, though—that would be factual, wouldn't it?"

"If it were true, yes."

"It's not?"

"There's no trail," he said, easing his car onto the road back to town. "These days most of my friends are married or hooked up. But no complaints." He decided a change in subject was in order. "I didn't buy food for dinner. I can see what I can find at the country store, but I'm not up for finding my way around Gran's kitchen. Every spoon and fork is tied to a memory. What if we have dinner at Knights Bridge village's one restaurant?"

"That sounds great," Clare said. "So much for my leftover mac and cheese."

"We can work on blowing up people's labels about us."

"By having a turkey club?"

He smiled at her. "And here I was thinking you'd be dancing on the tables."

"Do you think librarians don't dance on tables?"

"I'm sure some librarians do, but the label says they don't."

"You think I don't," she said.

"Do you?"

She laughed, watching out the passenger window as

they wound their way into the village. "Not since that one time in college."

"I will definitely have to hear about that."

"Have you ever danced on tables—or have you only goaded other people into doing it?"

He gave a mock shudder. "Dancing."

"You don't dance?"

"Only if given no other choice."

"It's good exercise, isn't it?"

"Excellent exercise," he said.

She sank into her seat and yawned. "Dancing could wake me up. I don't know why I'm so sleepy."

"Because you're having a good day," Logan said.

"Yes, I am."

When they arrived in the village, the white lights on their evergreen boughs were lit up against the darkening afternoon. "Not bad." He parked in front of the house. "But I've had enough decorating for one day, haven't you? Time for a walk and dinner."

"Sounds perfect."

SIX

➤ ←

"Spirit!" he cried... "hear me! I am not the man I
was. I will not be the man I must have been but
for this intercourse... Assure me that I yet may
change these shadows you have shown me, by an
altered life!"... The kind hand trembled.

–CHARLES DICKENS, *A CHRISTMAS CAROL*

CLARE'S HEAD WAS SPINNING BY EARLY EVE-
ning when she collected Owen at the Frosts' house, not
far from their mill and her apartment. A day of new experiences, to say the least.

Randy pulled her aside as Owen belted himself into
the backseat. "My wife suffered from severe anxiety for
a while—for too long. It started after our daughters were

in a car accident when they were teenagers. They were missing, trapped in the car, for a few hours. We couldn't find them." He bit the corner of his lip, clearly remembering. "It was tough. They weren't physically injured, but the emotional scars—Louise got where she wouldn't go out of town. She worried about every raindrop causing an accident. It crept up on her but she's doing great now."

"I'm glad to hear it," Clare said.

Randy narrowed his gaze on her. He didn't seem to notice the bite of the night cold. "I understand you lost your husband in a car accident. Black ice."

Clare nodded. "That's right."

"Had to be rough with Owen on the way. You're raising a happy boy, Clare. If you ever want to talk to Louise, she's here."

"Thank you. I've let…" She stopped, tried again. "The move affected me more than I realized. I don't want to live my life in fear, or put that on Owen."

"Understood." Randy grinned. "Now I'll butt out and mind my own business."

He opened the driver's door for her but she didn't get in. "Thanks again for taking care of Owen," she said, then smiled. "He's going to start lobbying me for a truck, but he won't win. I am not buying a truck."

Randy laughed. "Stick to your guns. Glad you got Daisy's house decorated."

"I was happy to help. I was under the impression that people in town didn't know Daisy's grandson well."

"The good Dr. Farrell? We don't."

"But you have an opinion about him?"

"He's a hell of a doctor."

Randy obviously didn't intend to go further. Clare slid in behind the wheel, and he shut the door for her, saying good-night to Owen. As predicted, her son regaled her with his reasons for needing a truck as they headed back to their sawmill apartment. She couldn't help but think of Logan alone at his grandmother's house. He was so smart, driven and confident that she couldn't imagine him worrying about ghosts. But Daisy had been born there, his father had grown up there and his grandfather had died there. As well as his grandmother's move had gone, it was a huge change. Being alone in a house with such memories—such a history—had to affect even a man who saw what Logan saw every day in his work.

Or not, Clare thought, following Owen up the steep stairs to their apartment. She'd left a light on in the living room. He was so tired he made no objection when she mentioned it was bedtime. As he yawned his way into the bathroom to brush his teeth, she pulled the cushions off the couch. She was tired, too—emotionally as well as physically.

Her emotional fatigue took her by surprise but there was no denying it was due to being around Logan. He hadn't looked particularly worried about ghosts or anything else over their simple dinner at Smith's, within walking distance of the Farrell house. The restaurant, in a converted house off the town common, was relatively crowded on a Saturday night, all their fellow diners local that Clare could see. She and Logan were both outsiders. At best she was a newcomer, and his deep roots in the area didn't matter since he'd never lived in town himself. Eric Sloan, Brandon's older brother, a Knights Bridge police officer, was there with his girlfriend, a paramedic—they'd all exchanged a few pleasantries. Clare was patient. She'd known it would take time to get to know people in her adopted town.

In any case, she'd been focused on Logan Farrell. If they'd signed up for a dating service, she was positive the computer would never have put their names together. Did she want to date a doctor? Absolutely not. Was she drawn to driven, high-achieving types? No. Was she interested in athletic men who couldn't sit still for five minutes? No. A man who knew he was sexy? No.

What kind of man *did* she want?

She pulled out the sofa bed, still made up from that

morning, and got her pillows out of the front closet. She paused, listening, but she could hear water running in the bathroom. She doubted Owen was getting into mischief.

She'd fallen head over heels for Stephen Morgan. Intelligent, ambitious, a lawyer who could handle himself in a courtroom but also knew how to fix things around the house. He'd been so excited about having a child. They'd known before he'd died they'd be having a baby boy.

Her family and friends had given her a year before encouraging her to start dating again. She'd tried an online dating service but had abandoned it after a month. *Get a social life, Clare, have some fun*, her friends would tell her. By *fun* they didn't necessarily mean sex, but they didn't necessarily not mean sex, either.

She sat on the thin mattress of her sofa bed. An image of herself in bed with Logan flashed in her mind. She shuddered, feeling a surge of warmth. Where had *that* come from? But she couldn't help wondering what it would be like with all his energy and drive focused on her, or at least on having sex with her.

She could do worse for a night or two.

But her attempt at humor—at dismissing her unbidden image—didn't work very well, and she was relieved when Owen came in, his shirt soaked and spattered with toothpaste. He grinned, and she could see the tooth she'd thought earlier in the week looked loose was, indeed, loose. Skating with the Sloan boys and checking out bird feeders with Randy Frost no doubt had helped.

"Come on," Clare said. "Hop up here. Let's read a story."

No more thinking about sex with Logan Farrell, at least not until the lights were out.

At 82 South Main Street on the Knights Bridge town common, Logan was awakening from the nightmare of his life. He leaped out of bed, heart racing, sweat pouring. His mind was filled with haunting images. He didn't know what, exactly, they were. Ghosts, maybe.

He swore he smelled smoke. Thick, black, acrid smoke.

He paused, standing on a hand-hooked rug. He didn't hear smoke alarms.

There's no damn smoke.

He breathed deeply, fully awake now. The smoke must have been part of his nightmare.

If he'd had Clare Morgan in bed with him, he wouldn't have had a nightmare.

He switched on the lamp on his bedside table. He looked around his father's old room at the matching bed frames, the bookcase, the prints of Boston and Cape Cod. His grandmother hadn't packed up any of the books. His father's old yearbooks; biographies of a few of the founding fathers, including George Washington, Thomas Jefferson, John Adams; more biographies of sports figures like Muhammad Ali, Lou Gehrig, a couple of race-car drivers Logan didn't recognize; and a row of classic novels, from *Sherlock Holmes* to *The Man in the Iron Mask* and *Where the Red Fern Grows.*

Logan hadn't paid attention to the furnishings or the contents of the room when he'd stayed here as a kid. He'd always been ready to go off with his grandfather to cut wood, plant the garden, sit in the fire trucks and talk to the firefighters. Tom Farrell hadn't been one to sit still, either.

But this room…

Logan felt his throat tighten with emotion. This was the room young Tom and Daisy Farrell had decorated for their son, now an aging man himself. They hadn't left the room as a shrine to him. They'd just never bothered changing it. New sheets and a fresh coat of paint every now and then, and it was set for guests—for their grandson. Logan's sister had stayed in another bedroom.

Everything would go soon, and new owners would do as they saw fit with the place.

His gaze settled on a framed photograph on the top shelf of the bookcase. It was taken at the Farrell farm, his father at around ten with his parents, the three of them standing in front of an apple tree laden with ripe fruit.

Another time, another life.

Logan went into the hall. He could see Clare with her slim hips and fair curls as she'd carried boxes down from the attic. Did she even know how pretty she was?

When was the last time she'd slept with a man?

He pushed *that* thought aside, but at least thinking about her had helped him shake off his nightmare.

Smoke and gunfire—and crying. He knew there'd been crying.

He grimaced and headed downstairs. His grandmother was a teetotaler, but his grandfather had imbibed every now and then. Logan smiled when he found a bottle of Jack Daniel's in the dining room. He was normally a Scotch drinker, but a good sour-mash whiskey would do fine after a nightmare and imagining himself in bed with Clare Morgan.

He splashed some of the whiskey in a glass and took it into the living room. He sat by the unlit fireplace and held up his glass. "Cheers, Grandpa. I miss you."

An hour later, when a colleague and friend at the ER called, Logan was all too eager to answer his phone. He answered questions about a patient he'd seen during the week and then waited for the expected shoe to drop. "We need you in here in the morning, Logan. Can you do it?"

"What time?"

"Ten. Eleven at the latest."

He looked at the shadows in the living room. "Yeah," he said. "I can be there."

"Where are you now?"

"I'm hanging out with the Ghost of Christmas Past."

His friend made no comment.

After Logan disconnected, he checked his whiskey glass. He'd had something like eight sips. He wasn't drunk. He wouldn't be hungover in the morning—which, he decided, couldn't come soon enough.

He wasn't going back to his bedroom.

"Hell, no."

He found an afghan one of Gran's friends had given her—she wasn't a knitter—and stretched out on the couch, wishing he'd found a way to have Clare with him. It was selfish and shallow of him, maybe, but he'd have made it worth her while.

Downright arrogant of him, he knew, but there it was.

He was in a kind of survival mode, and a good-hearted, attractive blonde would have kept the nightmares and ghosts at bay, at least for tonight.

By daylight, Logan had shrugged off his bad night. Since he had to be on his way as soon as possible, he drove rather than walked to Smith's, open early for breakfast. Yesterday's relatively balmy temperatures had fallen off the table overnight. According to his phone, it was nine degrees. In his world, that was cold. Among the Sloans, it probably wasn't bad. Three of them were gathered at a table, coffees already in front of them and their breakfasts ordered.

Christopher Sloan, one of two full-time Knights Bridge firefighters and the youngest of the five brothers, motioned to an empty chair. "Feel free to join us, Dr. Farrell."

"Logan," he said, taking a seat, if only because it seemed rude to turn down the invitation and sit alone. "Morning. Cold out there."

"It's December," Justin said with a shrug of his broad shoulders. He was the second eldest, the ostensible heir to running Sloan & Sons, the family's construction business.

"Either way," Logan said, "coffee is in order."

Eric, the eldest Sloan and a police officer, called over the waitress. "Our good doctor needs coffee. Know what you're having for breakfast, Logan?"

"I thought I'd try the oat waffles—with blackberry preserves on the side, please. No syrup."

Eric made a face. "Waffles without syrup. Suit yourself."

Logan put in his order. The waitress, a local woman, delivered his coffee in a heavy diner-style mug. The Sloans asked him about decorating his grandmother's house and her move into assisted living. He quickly realized they knew far more about what was going on in his life than he did about their lives.

He also realized they didn't approve of him. It wasn't anything overt—not as it had been yesterday with Randy Frost. But it was there, the whiff of "we know you're a heartless bastard." Logan figured their judgment, fair or unfair, had more to do with their ideas about doctors, city doctors, people who lived in the city—any or all of the above. That didn't bother him so much, since they didn't know him well and he was what he was. What got to him—and took him by surprise—was the Sloans' faint but unmistakable suspicion of his motives for being in their town, helping his grandmother.

"Daisy's beloved in town," Christopher said. "Every firefighter who's served in the town fire department as a professional or a volunteer would do anything for her. A lot of firefighters from neighboring towns would, too."

"Good to know," Logan said.

Christopher wasn't done yet. "Your grandfather's a legend in the area. I don't know if he saved as many lives as you have in the ER, but he saved quite a number during his years with the department. He also prevented injuries and deaths with inspections, education, drills. He wasn't a hot dog who got a rise out of fighting a big fire."

"It's good to know he's well remembered," Logan said, drinking some of his coffee.

"He stayed active after he retired," Eric said. "Right up until the end. Losing him was hard on Daisy. She didn't want to give him up."

"I know she didn't," Logan said. "None of us did."

"The two of them had a good run," Justin added.

Logan nodded. "They did. I'm glad you three think so well of her. She likes company. I'm sure she'd welcome visitors."

"Tom never wanted to go into assisted living," Christopher said.

The Sloan breakfasts arrived. Eggs, bacon, a mound of home fries, toast dripping with butter. They'd probably burn it off before noon. Logan thought he was beginning to understand their ambivalence toward him. "It was her idea to move," he said. "She was lonely at home, and the house became too much for her, even with assistance. She wants to sell it. We want her to be content and safe, and to respect her wishes, of course."

"So it was her decision to move," Eric said, obviously skeptical.

"Yes, and it's one we all support. That it's a choice instead of a necessity helps." Logan's breakfast arrived—even a short stack of waffles was more than he would eat in one sitting. "My grandfather isn't here. I wish he were. Gran has to make her own decisions."

"He didn't make decisions for her," Christopher said. "He wasn't that kind of guy."

"I know. They made their decisions together. But we're all aware she'd never have gone into assisted living if he were still alive, and we'd have found a way to make that happen if at all possible."

"Our grandmother's still on her own," Justin said. "She says she'll walk into the woods on a cold night and go to sleep before she'll move into assisted living."

"She has a bad attitude," Eric said with a grin.

"I get where you're coming from," Logan said, spreading a glob of melting butter over his waffles. In for a penny, in for a pound, he thought. "You all live in town. You know my grandmother and knew my grandfather well. In some ways, better than I ever could, since I've never lived in Knights Bridge."

"You don't come around much," Christopher said.

"Not in recent years, no."

"Are you sure Daisy isn't telling you what you want to hear?"

"There's no way to know for certain. I am sure she is clear on her options and has chosen the one she believes is best for her."

Eric dipped a fork into his eggs. "That's a careful answer."

"I'm not asking you to trust me," Logan said, keeping any edge out of his tone. "Talk to her yourself if you'd like."

Justin leaned back in his chair. "Didn't we throw you into the Frosts' millpond once or twice?"

Logan picked up the small dish of blackberry preserves. "Once," he said. "It was some sort of game, as I recall."

Justin grinned. "Beating up on the city boy."

Logan grinned back at him. "That must have been it. The water was damn cold."

"Always is," Eric said.

"That was before my time," Christopher said, softening slightly. "Tom was proud of you, Logan. His grandson, the doctor."

Logan stuffed a forkful of waffles in his mouth, hoping it kept the Sloans from noticing he had a lump in his throat. His nightmare came back at him with its screams and smell of smoke. Had he somehow channeled his grandfather—fires he'd fought, chaos and fears he'd endured?

The Sloans were watching him. Logan spread the preserves on his waffles.

"Oh, man," Eric said, "I don't think I can watch."

Justin and Christopher grinned and teased their eldest brother about what a wimp he was, and Logan relaxed. These were men who were accustomed to teasing and confrontation. Their suspicion could die down as quickly as it had flared up.

"I appreciate your concern for my grandmother," Logan said.

"No problem," Eric said. "We do our best to look out for her."

"It can be hard to know what's best when someone you care about is in the sunset of their life. You wish…" Logan cut his waffles with his fork. "You wish you had more time and you know you don't."

The three brothers were silent a moment. Finally Justin stabbed his home fries with his fork. "You must see all kinds of tragedies in your work. You have to know how to distance yourself in order to do your job. I'm glad I work with two-by-fours and nail guns."

"Always good to have a two-by-four at hand when dealing with a Sloan," Christopher said with a grin. "Especially one of the first-borns."

Eric rolled his eyes. "So says the spoiled little brother. Speaking of younger brothers, I understand Brandon took Owen Morgan skating yesterday with his boys while Clare helped you decorate Daisy's house."

"They seemed to have a good time," Logan said, keeping his tone neutral.

"Then they made snowmen together. Winter in a small town, right?" Eric lifted his coffee mug. "Owen's got you and our new librarian paired up. He told Brandon. Thought you might want to know."

"Clare's new in town," Logan said. "Do you watch out for her, too?"

Eric didn't hesitate. "Count on it."

After breakfast, Logan got in his car and immediately wished he'd just grabbed coffee and headed straight to Boston. The sky had turned blue, the air clear and sharp and not much warmer than when he'd left for Smith's. Conversation with the Sloans had shifted to topics less fraught with emotional peril, such as who was doing horse-drawn sleigh and wagon rides for Christmas. Logan had never done either and had no plans to. But he didn't tell the Sloans that. They'd gone from open suspicion bordering on hostility to grudging neutrality. He understood. He couldn't do enough for his grandmother. No one could.

He stopped to see her on his way out of town. She was in her apartment, sitting in her comfy chair, pencil in hand as she worked a large-print crossword puzzle. "What's a six-letter word for sheep stew? No one says sheep stew. Lamb stew, but it's four letters. I've never liked lamb."

"Do you want me to tell you if I know?"

"Yes, why do you think I asked? I have a whole book of puzzles. Hundreds of words I need to think up. I'm not a slacker if I get help with one."

Logan smiled. "Mutton."

"Ah. Of course. Ugh, though. I had mutton in Ireland. I hated it."

"When did you go to Ireland?"

"I went with your grandfather—oh, I don't remember the exact year. It was after your father graduated from college, because we didn't have two nickels to put together until then. Tom's people came to the Swift River Valley from Northern Ireland in the eighteenth century. We visited it and the republic. We had the best time."

"Good memories, Gran."

"We could have spent the money on a new kitchen. I'm glad we didn't. I'd rather have the memories." She pointed her pencil at him. "Except for the mutton."

"Gran…"

"Hold on. Let me write mutton before I forget."

He waited. She had the most energy and was most alert in the morning and planned accordingly. Once she finished writing her word in the appropriate spaces, she put her pencil on top of the crossword puzzle on her lap and looked at him expectantly.

"I have to go," he said. "I have to be at the hospital in a couple of hours."

"Oh, my goodness. Was there a bus accident or something? Not a shooting, I hope."

"There's no mass casualty incident, Gran. It's normal scheduling issues. I'm sorry I have to run, but I'll get back here as soon as I can. It's not far. I'll call you."

She narrowed her aged eyes on him. "Do not feel guilty, Logan Farrell. I'm *fine*."

"Clare Morgan and I got a good start on the house. Her son thinks we should put up a Christmas tree. It would be a nice touch to have a tree lit up in a window. We could even put one up on the porch."

"Whatever you decide will be perfect."

He kissed her on the top of her head. "You're the best, Gran. Call me if you need anything."

"I think I'll like taking yoga. I wasn't sure I would. I was just humoring Audrey Frost. Do you think I'm up for regular classes?"

"What do you think?"

"I suppose it'll be all right. I can't imagine they'd have us do headstands."

He laughed. "Listen to your body and your doctor."

"And here I am sniffing at ninety."

Logan left her contemplating her yoga classes and returning to her crossword puzzle.

He hated getting back in his car, but he knew he had to. As he wound his way out of town, he wondered what Clare and her son were doing this morning. Making pancakes? Sleeping late?

When he hit the highway east to Boston, Logan forced them to the back of his mind.

Two and a half hours later, when he walked into the emergency department, he was focused on his job and nothing else.

A Recipe for Oat Waffles

→ ←

*Who doesn't like waffles on a cold winter morning? Made
with traditional rolled oats, these waffles are both hearty
and light. Making maple syrup is one of the early signs
of spring in New England, but waffles with homemade
strawberry or blackberry preserves are also irresistible.
There's nothing like opening a jar of homemade blackberry
jam on a cold winter morning. It tastes like summer.*

3 tablespoons butter
1¼ cups all-purpose flour
1¼ cups water
¾ cup rolled oats
1 tablespoon sugar
½ teaspoon baking soda
1½ teaspoons baking powder
¼ teaspoon salt
1 to 1¼ cups buttermilk
2 eggs

1. Combine oats and water in a saucepan and simmer for about
   3 minutes, stirring occasionally. Add butter, stirring until it
   melts. Sift together remaining dry ingredients and set aside.
   In a separate bowl, beat lightly together eggs and buttermilk, then stir in oatmeal and butter mixture. Add dry ingredients just until blended.

2. Preheat waffle iron and use about ¾ cup batter per 8-inch
   waffle. Makes four. Serve with butter and pure maple syrup
   or your favorite preserves.

SEVEN

→ ←

"You have never seen the like of me before!"
exclaimed the Spirit.

–Charles Dickens, *A Christmas Carol*

WHEN CLARE ARRIVED AT DAISY FARRELL'S
house, she had mentally arranged the window boxes on
the front porch and knew more or less what she wanted
to do. She had enlisted Owen's help snipping boughs
from a huge white pine that stood on the corner of the
parking lot at Frost Millworks. She planned to use them
in the boxes, and she'd found ribbons in her gift-packing
materials that she could try out to see what worked best.

As she mounted the porch steps, she admitted to a
flutter in her stomach at the thought of seeing Logan

again. Her dreams last night hadn't helped. She didn't even want to think about the details with Owen behind her, trotting innocently onto the porch. She didn't see Logan's car but assumed he was off doing errands.

Eric Sloan walked by in his police uniform and called a hello to her and Owen. "Working on the place on your own today?" he asked her.

She shook her head. "We're meeting Logan."

"He must not have been able to reach you—he had to go to Boston. He was called in to the ER at the last minute. It happens."

"Right. Of course. It's no big deal. Owen and I can do up the window boxes on our own."

Her feigned cheerfulness didn't seem to convince Eric. "The place looks good," he said. "Daisy will be pleased."

"I hope so. Thanks for stopping by."

"No problem."

Clare waited until he was out of sight before she checked her phone, but she didn't have a voice mail or text from Logan. She couldn't remember if she'd given him her email address, but there was no email from him, either.

She had his contact information and debated calling or texting him, but if he was at work…

And he'd left without getting in touch with her, hadn't he?

She put her phone back in her pocket, regretting letting herself get excited about seeing him. What had she been thinking, getting ahead of herself like that? She knew better. It wasn't as if she wasn't familiar with his type.

Logan Farrell took care of Logan Farrell.

"Let's unload the car," she told Owen. "It's cold out but we're dressed for the weather. We can make quick work of the window boxes."

"Can we have hot chocolate again?" her son asked.

"We can have lunch at Smith's. They'll have hot chocolate."

"Logan can come, too."

"Logan isn't here." She heard the sharpness in her voice and forced herself to soften it as she continued. "He's a busy doctor in Boston. Come on. Let's keep moving so we don't turn into Popsicles."

Owen giggled at the idea of them turning into Popsicles. They ran back down the steps and out to her car. She handed him the small bag of ribbons to carry and grabbed the pine boughs for herself.

"Look," he said when they reached the front porch. "There's a *present*."

Clare hadn't noticed the small box on the doormat before. "That's nice, Owen, but it's not for us."

"It is. Look. That's my name. *O-w-e-n*."

She set the boughs on the floor next to the front door. Sure enough, a small envelope attached to the box was addressed to "Clare & Owen." Owen's name was printed. Hers was a nearly illegible scrawl. She pulled off her gloves and opened the envelope.

Inside was a handwritten note on lined paper out of a tablet she'd noticed yesterday in Daisy's kitchen. The note had obviously been jotted in haste, in the same scrawl as her name:

Clare, my apologies. I have to run. Work calls. I'd have called you but it was early and I didn't want to disturb you. I was looking forward to today. Door is unlocked. I figure it's safe. Help yourself to Gran's books and feel free to do whatever decorating you want to do. My best to Owen.
Logan

Owen was ripping open the box. Inside was an old-fashioned snow globe with a scene of Santa and his elves at the North Pole. Logan must have found it in the decorations. Owen shook it, and snow fell on the quaint scene. He'd never seen one before and was transfixed.

"That's from Logan," Clare said.

"It's so cool."

She felt like a heel for having jumped to conclusions.

She pushed open the front door, and she and Owen went inside. The house was reasonably warm. Logan must not have turned the heat down when he left. Owen bee-lined for the kitchen, where the owner's grandson had set out the tin of Dutch cocoa and a clean saucepan on the counter. Clare was careful about too much sugar, but it *was* a cold morning.

It wouldn't be the day she'd planned, but she'd make it a good one.

By early afternoon, Clare had finished rearranging the window boxes to her satisfaction, and Owen was bored. She'd save sorting through more of Daisy's boxes of books for when he wasn't with her. She and Owen settled into the kitchen, where she made hot chocolate, trying to picture Tom and Daisy Farrell's life here. Had they ever wanted to live anywhere else? Had it even been possible?

Clare ran her fingertips over the worn counter. The old house was a gem, but it did need a significant amount of work. She let herself imagine being in charge of ren-ovations. What would she do? What colors would she use—what style would she go with for new furnishings? It would be fun to live in town. She could walk to work and Owen could walk to school and to visit his friends.

A cold draft brought her out of her thoughts.

The back door was cracked open. How had that happened? The wind? But it was a still day, almost no wind to speak of.

Old houses, she thought.

"Okay, Owen, time to head home," she said, turning from the counter. She expected to find him at the table, but he wasn't there. She went into the dining room, figuring he was checking for more treasures among Daisy's things.

He wasn't there, either.

Clare felt her heart jolt. "Owen!" she yelled, remembering the draft.

She ran back into the kitchen and out through the back door onto the landing, hitting an icy patch. She stopped abruptly, spotting her son on the walk that led across the yard to the driveway and unattached garage.

He grinned at her, the picture of innocence. "Hi, Mom."

She tried to calm her heart rate. "Owen, what are you doing out here?"

"I'm leaving bread for the birds."

Sure enough, he'd crumbled and scattered bread crumbs on the walk. Clare didn't see any birds, but something would find the crumbs before long. Owen had on his boots and his hat, but no gloves and, worse, no coat.

"That's great," she said, "but you need to wear a coat when it's this cold."

"I'm coming right back in."

"And you need to tell me when you're going outside."

He blinked at her. "Didn't you see me?"

"No, I didn't. You can't count on that. You need to ask permission."

"When I'm bigger can I go outside without asking?"

She relaxed, trying not to look as if she'd panicked. "Yes, but it's always good to let people know where you are. Logan couldn't be here today, and he left us a note. That was his way of letting us know. Because you're six, it's a matter of safety, but it's also good manners."

"Okay. What kind of birds will eat the bread?"

"I don't know. Maybe we'll see some while we pack up. Birds probably won't come with us standing here. I'm getting cold."

He smiled. "Me, too."

They went back inside. Clare engaged Owen's help to clean up the kitchen. He was clearly preoccupied with his crumbs for the birds. "Let's put our coats on," she said. "We can go out front and take pictures of our window boxes."

"Can we send them to Logan?"

She'd been thinking more along the lines of showing

them to Daisy Farrell on her next trip out to Rivendell. But Owen looked so eager. "Sure. I have his number."

They bundled up and went back out to the front porch. She took a few shots of their handiwork and let Owen take a few, and he picked out the two best ones to send to Logan. Clare took a moment to formulate her text. She felt ridiculously self-conscious. She was a professional librarian accustomed to dealing with all sorts of people under every manner of circumstance, if not this particular person and this particular circumstance.

Finally she typed a quick message. Owen is very proud of our boxes.

She didn't expect an immediate answer, or an answer at all, particularly since Logan was at the ER. But he answered before she could put her phone back in her pocket: Perfect. Tell Owen thanks.

I will. Thank you for the snow globe.

Sorry I'm not there.

Me, too.

Clare hit send before she realized what she'd typed. She turned off her phone to keep from embarrassing herself further. Surely Logan was too busy to respond.

It was the adrenaline dump from Owen's escapade, she told herself. She wasn't thinking before she acted.

"Mom, your face is red," Owen said.

"It's this cold weather. Let's go home and laze around the house. How does that sound? We can do laundry and get ready for school tomorrow."

He had to check on his bread crumbs first. They were still scattered on the walk in the cold. Clare assured him they would be gone before he returned, which he vowed to do tomorrow after school.

"Not alone," Clare said.

"You can come with me. Right, Mom?"

She smiled. "Absolutely."

When they arrived at their sawmill apartment, Louise Frost came down from the Frost mill and met them at the entrance. Water rushed over the dam, but more ice had formed with the colder temperatures. "I love the sound of water," Louise said. "It's soothing. Some say that being close to water is good for the spirits. Ions or something."

"Really? That doesn't surprise me. I wish I could open the windows and listen to the water at night."

"That's one of the perks of being here in summer. I can feel the cold rising up from the water. A good day for soup. Randy and I spent the afternoon cooking after we got back from church. We made chicken-and-vegetable soup. We put some aside and thought you and Owen might like it." She held up a large glass Mason jar. "Soup was always a good way to get my girls to eat vegetables."

"Thank you so much," Clare said. "Owen and I both love soup."

Louise nodded up toward the Frost mill. "I was in my office just now working on travel plans. It's not work-work. Randy and I are going to Europe this spring. I swear planning's half the fun. Have you ever been?"

"I did a semester in Paris in college."

"Oh, my. That sounds wonderful. For a long time, I was afraid to travel. I didn't want to drive to the airport never mind get on a plane. It got so I didn't want to leave town. Just thinking about it set off a panic attack. And my daughters…" She shuddered. "I must have driven them crazy with my anxiety. It was bad, but I rational-ized it. My family and friends indulged me. Everyone walked on eggshells to keep me from flipping out."

"I'm so glad you're doing well now," Clare said.

"Me, too. I still have to work at it. At least I've stopped blaming myself. Randy told me he mentioned the girls' car accident to you. I was always prone to anxiety, but after that—well, it got worse and worse and blossomed into a full-blown anxiety disorder. Therapy and medica-tion helped. I'm done with both. Clare, you know what I'm saying, don't you?"

"Get help if I need it."

She nodded. "You don't have to suffer and you don't have to let anxiety spiral out of control. You can control it instead of it controlling you. A year ago I wouldn't drive to Worcester. Now I'm booking flights to Amsterdam. They say Schiphol's a great airport for first-time travelers to Europe. Great location, well run, everything is in English and everyone speaks English—although I've bought a Dutch-English dictionary. I think my pronunciation must be awful, though." She smiled, then tapped a finger onto the lid of the Mason jar in Clare's arms. "It's good with biscuits or corn muffins."

"Thank you, Louise," Clare said. "For the soup and for your story."

Once upstairs in her apartment, Clare put the soup in the refrigerator and stood at the window overlooking the millpond and falls. If Owen sneaked out here, he could get into real trouble, fast. She kept the downstairs and the apartment doors locked, but he could unlock them if he put his mind to it. What she had to do, she knew, was take appropriate precautions, keep an eye on him and trust him. Trust that she was teaching him well. He'd put on his boots before sneaking out that morning, right? And he hadn't gone out to the road or run off to see the Sloan boys.

She could put the brakes on turning into an overprotective, anxiety-driven mother.

She wouldn't go as far as Louise Frost had gone.

Keeping an eye on Owen would be easier with two sets of eyes, but she was used to being an only parent. Her own parents—and his paternal grandparents—saw him often, giving her breaks. And giving Owen a break from her, too. But they were used to their lives together, just the two of them.

Laundry, soup, reading. A perfect winter afternoon and evening.

Clare pulled off her coat and hung it on one of a row of pegs by the door. She took her phone out of her pocket and turned it on before she remembered her impulsive text to Logan.

He'd responded. I'll be back this week. See you then.

She tried not to read anything into it. He'd left a few things unfinished at his grandmother's house. He had to wrap it all up. He would want Daisy to get on with putting the house up for sale, but he could help from Boston. Find someone to clear out anything she and the rest of the Farrell family didn't want, clean, paint and stage the place. He could afford it, and delegating made sense given his busy life in Boston.

She didn't respond to his text. It'd been a couple of hours, and responding now wasn't necessary and would look as if she were thinking up reasons to be in touch with him—and she wasn't fourteen with a crush on a cute high school senior.

She picked out *The Night Before Christmas* to read to Owen, then gathered up dirty linens and got him to bring his laundry to the stacked washer and dryer in the kitchen. This was her life now, she thought, and it was good.

Librarian that she was, Clare knew how to immerse herself in details and research, and by Friday, she had read a dozen local newspaper articles mentioning Tom Farrell and his work with the fire department. The man had enjoyed quite a career, and he was well respected for his pioneering work with small-town fire safety and firefighting. Daisy, his longtime wife, had been a homemaker, always at his side—and he at hers.

Clare unearthed a notice of the Farrells' wedding in 1948, when Daisy was eighteen and Tom was twenty. A small, grainy black-and-white photograph depicted the happy couple. Clare found herself staring at Daisy's smile, her dark, neatly curled hair and her smooth, unwrinkled skin. She'd been so young. Did she remember anymore what she'd looked like then?

Logan bore a strong resemblance to Tom Farrell, Clare thought as she'd stared at the wedding photo. Tom was a good fifteen years younger on his wedding day than his grandson was now, but the resemblance was unmistakable.

She walked down South Main to the Farrell house. It wasn't five o'clock but it was already dark, the days noticeably shorter as December took hold in southern New England. Seasonal lights twinkled cheerfully on the businesses, churches and houses on the common. Skaters, some of them arm-in-arm, glided across the ice, glowing under the multicolored lights on a trio of evergreens.

As transfixed as she was by the beautiful New England scene, Clare felt tears rising in her eyes. She was an outsider in Knights Bridge and probably always would be. Logan hadn't grown up in the small town, either, but he had roots here, a greater sense of belonging. Even if people had questions about him, they accepted him as one of their own.

It was the lure and the challenge of a small town, wasn't it? Part of the appeal of Knights Bridge was that sense of place, of home. But was it possible for a newcomer? Did having roots in one of the lost Quabbin towns make a difference?

Overthinking.

Clare smiled to herself. *Overthinking* was an alarm-bell word for her. It warned her she was propelling herself too far into the future and trying to read minds. She didn't actually know what anyone in Knights Bridge thought of her or Logan.

As promised, Maggie Sloan was waiting on the Farrell front porch, sitting on the porch rail next to the evergreen boughs. She didn't have her boys and Owen with her. Clare glanced around, but she was positive they weren't there. She'd have heard them. "Maggie, aren't you catering an event tonight? I can take the boys. Really, it's not a problem. I can sort books while the boys play."

Maggie shook her head. "Sorting books can wait. Even if there's a first edition tucked in one of Daisy's boxes, it's been there for a while. It's not going anywhere." She smiled as she eased off the porch rail. "I thought you could join me."

"Help you cater? I'd love to, but I've never done any catering."

"You don't have to do a thing. You can ride out there with me in the van. No, I meant join me for the event. I'm catering but I'm also attending. It sounds more complicated than it is."

Clare wasn't sure anything was too complicated for Maggie. "Are you sure? If I'm not invited…"

"*I'm* inviting you. It's at Carriage Hill. Girls' night. Olivia, Jess Frost, Samantha Bennett, Heather Sloan, Adrienne Portale—who am I missing? My sisters can't be there. Phoebe's still off with Noah and the twins are in graduate school in New York. I'll be there, of course. I insisted on catering because Heather wanted to cook."

"Your sister-in-law," Clare said, trying to keep the names straight.

Maggie grinned. "Give Heather a hammer and she's fine. Don't let her near a whisk and a mixing bowl. She's a menace in the kitchen. If anyone deserves five older brothers, it's Heather. You'll love her. You've met Samantha, right?"

"Treasure hunter and pirate expert. She stops by the library often."

"She and my brother-in-law Justin are engaged. Long story. On paper you'd never put them together. In real life, they're perfect for each other. Adrienne is a wine enthusiast house-sitting for a retired diplomat. The Sloans are renovating his house on Echo Lake. You've met Olivia and Jessica. Olivia owns the Farm at Carriage Hill."

"And Jessica works at Frost Millworks and is married to Mark Flanagan, a local architect."

"You see? You fit right in. Dylan, Olivia's fiancé, is vacating the premises for the evening. I think he and some of the guys are meeting at Justin's old cider mill and building a bonfire."

"If Brandon wants to join them, I can take care of the boys."

Maggie shook her head. "He's fine. There will be other bonfires. Those are his words." She tilted her head back, scrutinizing Clare. "We both agree you need a night out and a chance to get to know people in town. Time to throttle back for an evening."

"You won't believe me if I tell you that sorting through boxes of musty books is my idea of throttling back?"

Maggie didn't hesitate. "No."

They walked to her house around the corner. Brandon Sloan had the three boys making pizza. Owen loved the idea of staying with his friends for the evening. Pepperoni, tomato sauce, cheese, movies and masculine energy. What was not to like for a six-year-old boy?

Maggie whisked Clare into her van, and off they went to the Farm at Carriage Hill. Olivia Frost's 1803 center-chimney house was out of a storybook, tastefully decorated for Christmas. Maggie parked by a sign with the inn's signature logo of blossoming chives, created by Olivia, a graphic designer.

"Brandon keeps threatening to plan a guys' night out that I can cater. It'd be easy. Beer, chips and salsa at a bonfire. They'd probably settle just for beer."

Clare laughed. "You could go all out and add guacamole."

"Brandon would say I'm underestimating him and his friends. Point is, they aren't hard to please. It's a quality

I've come to appreciate more than I used to." She started to push open her door. "Coming back home to Knights Bridge has been a fresh start for me. I don't mean to be presumptuous—well, maybe I do—but I've had the impression that part of the reason you took the job at the library was to make a fresh start for yourself. You know. Draw a line under the past and find yourself a man."

"Maggie…"

"That's not why I came back, you understand. I already had a man. I was just incredibly mad at him." She smiled, her turquoise eyes shining. "All water over the dam."

Clare bit her lip. "Does everyone in town think I'm here to find a man?"

"I don't know. I haven't asked everyone. I haven't asked anyone, actually. But am I wrong?"

"I wanted to move out of the city with Owen, and Knights Bridge is close to my parents."

"Right." Maggie sounded dubious. "It's a practical choice."

"For one kind of fresh start. There are more single men in Boston. If that was my priority, I'd have stayed, wouldn't I?"

"Not if you needed to escape memories in order to start dating again. Look, I'm sorry. I'm being really, really blunt and I haven't even had a glass of wine—which is my quota when I'm driving. You, however, aren't driving. Kick back, relax and have a good time tonight." Maggie smiled cheerfully. "You're among friends."

They went into the house through the main door and entered a living room with a roaring fire in the center-chimney fireplace. Maggie made introductions as they all helped get the food out of the van and set it up in the dining room. Adrienne Portale poured wine, and the evening got underway.

Great food, drinks, a beautiful home on the edge of the Quabbin wilderness and new women friends. Clare smiled as she sipped a lovely merlot.

What was not to like for a thirty-two-year-old widow?

EIGHT

Uncle Scrooge had imperceptibly become so gay
and light of heart, that he would have pledged
the unconscious company in return...if the Ghost
had given him time.

–Charles Dickens, *A Christmas Carol*

THE BOYS WERE STILL UP, BUT BARELY,
when Maggie and Clare returned. Brandon had set out
sleeping bags on the living room floor, and the boys
were tucked in, watching a movie as they fought to stay
awake. Clare tiptoed into the living room to say good-
night to her son.

"Mom," Owen whispered, snuggled into his sleeping
bag, "guess who else is here."

"Who?" she asked, matching his whisper.

His eyes widened with excitement. *"Logan."*

Brandon was standing in the doorway. "Logan stopped by before dinner. I told him he could join us for pizza if he didn't badger me about putting broccoli or avocados or something on it."

Clare tried to conceal her surprise. "He's in town?"

"He's in the kitchen."

"Clare's had wine," Maggie said.

Brandon came into the living room. "No driving?"

Maggie shook her head. "Not a good idea."

"I'm not…" Clare glanced at Owen, then looked back at Brandon and Maggie. "Two and a half glasses of a Kendrick Winery merlot, plus far too much of Maggie's excellent cooking. I could have eaten all the molasses cookies by myself."

"It's a recipe I got from Daisy Farrell," Maggie said. "'Tis the season for cookies."

"'Tis the season for a lot of indulgences, apparently," Brandon said.

Logan entered the living room from the wide, open doorway to the dining room. "You two have a house full," he said, addressing Maggie and Brandon. "There's lots of room at my grandmother's house. Clare can stay there."

Her head was spinning and not just with wine. Owen

yawned, clearly settled in for the evening. Aidan and Tyler were both almost asleep. Maggie, too, was done in for the night, leaning against her husband, his arm over her shoulders. The polite option, Clare knew, was to make her exit. But Maggie was right about her capacity to drive.

It was hard enough to think straight around Logan even when she hadn't had wine. He collected his jacket off the back of a chair and steered her outside as they both said good-night to Maggie, Brandon and the boys.

The cold air jolted Clare into at least stopping herself from sinking into Logan as they walked up Maggie and Brandon's quiet street to South Main. She tried to formulate a coherent thought. It wasn't just the merlot muddling her. It was fatigue, the energy of the women at Carriage Hill, the proximity of this man—this hard-driving, perplexing man.

"I could pass a sobriety test," she said, defiant.

"Ah-ha."

"You sound skeptical."

"More than skeptical, I hope. Want to try walking a straight line?"

"No. I want to get warm."

"That we can do."

There was something in his voice that reminded her he wasn't a married neighbor or a brother or uncle. She felt safe with him but that didn't mean she needed to be talking about getting warm.

"I know you don't have to be falling-down drunk to be unfit to drive," she said, fighting a yawn. "I am fit to walk, though. You won't have to carry me."

"That's good."

"I mean—" She stopped herself. "Never mind."

They came to his grandmother's house. He'd turned on the lights they'd strung, adding to the festive feel as well as lighting their way on the walk and steps up to the porch. "You did a great job with the window boxes," he said as he opened the door. "Thank you."

"Owen helped."

"He's a great kid."

The house was warm, a floor lamp on by the fireplace in the front room adding a romantic glow. Or maybe it was the merlot making everything seem romantic, Clare thought. Logan helped her with her coat. The brush of his hand on the back of her neck felt romantic, too. When had she allowed herself to have such reactions? Romance was for other people. It was no longer for her.

And it was dangerous, especially with a man like Logan Farrell.

She didn't want to be his latest adrenaline rush. The "mustn't touch" widow and single mother. The new library director in his family's hometown. He already had a reputation in Knights Bridge. Why not push it to its limits? She wasn't a Sloan, a Frost or an O'Dunn, but people in town wouldn't want her hurt by a man like Logan. By any man, really.

"Gran left lemon-chamomile tea," he said, breaking through her fog of thoughts.

She stared at him blankly. "Tea?"

He smiled. "I'll put on the kettle."

She did not walk a straight line into the kitchen. It wasn't just the wine—it was being here, with Logan Farrell making her tea. And it was fatigue. She didn't know if she'd last through tea.

"Chamomile tea will help settle your stomach and relax you," he said as he stood at the sink and ran water into a stainless-steel kettle. "The tea bags look reasonably fresh."

"I never would have expected your grandmother to have herbal teas."

"People can surprise you."

Clare smiled, sinking onto a chair at the table. "Yes, they can. I know that from my work."

He set the kettle on the stove and turned on the heat under it. "I'm sorry I didn't let you know I was heading into town. I finished my shift and got out of town."

"You don't owe me advance notice."

"Imagine if you'd come back ten minutes later and decided to sleep here for the same reasons you're here now. Wine, night out on the town, full house at the Sloans'." He opened a canister on the counter. "You could have walked in and found me dozing on the couch or chasing ghosts in the attic."

Clare tried not to picture herself walking in on him. "It would have been presumptuous of me to spend the night here without your permission."

"Practical," he said, examining a tea bag. "Anyway, what's wrong with being presumptuous under the circumstances? Better than camping out with six-year-olds."

"Maggie or Brandon would have given me a ride home."

"This is more fun, isn't it?" He set a tea bag into each of two mugs. "I'm not criticizing you."

"Just being hospitable?"

"Trying. You haven't slipped between Gran's guest sheets yet. They're like sandpaper."

"Not like your 500-thread-count sheets at home?"

He glanced back at her with a grin. "Mock me, Clare Morgan. Wait until your delicate skin and Gran's sheets make contact."

"You're assuming I sleep in the nude, when in fact…" She jolted upright, almost falling off her chair. "I didn't just say that, did I?"

"That I assume you sleep in the nude? No, you didn't. I try not to make too many assumptions, at least unfounded ones. I didn't see you walk in here with an overnight bag." He reached for the kettle. "If you have head-to-toe flannel pajamas, they're not here, are they?"

"I don't have head-to-toe flannel pajamas." She smiled, recovering herself. "I have a head-to-toe flannel nightgown."

"There's a range of flannel. Everything from lightweight, flowing flannel to your basic Paul Bunyan nightshirt."

"Think the Grinch in his red nightshirt."

"You don't make that easy."

"Scrooge?"

Logan shuddered. "Don't mention Scrooge."

"Why, have you had a visit from the ghost of Jacob Marley in his leg irons and chains?"

Logan didn't answer, instead pouring the boiling water into the two mugs. He brought them to the table and sat across from her. "Back to your flannel nightshirt."

"I see how it is. It's easier for you to get other people to talk than to talk yourself. Do you have a favorite movie rendition of *A Christmas Carol*?"

"Not going to tell me more about your nightshirt, are you?"

"I'm getting my second wind. I'm not talking to you

about sheets, nightshirts or anything to do with how I'm spending the night." But she heard her words and made a face. "I'm not helping my case. Was it the spirit of Christmas Past, Present or Yet to Come who got to you?"

Logan picked up his tea and took a sip. "The lemon helps the chamomile, doesn't it? Cuts the I'm-drinking-weeds taste."

"You, Dr. Farrell, are changing the subject."

"You noticed."

"Doctors like to fix things, don't they? Especially ER doctors."

"We do our best."

"But not everything that comes through your doors can be fixed," she said quietly, staring at her chamomile tea. She couldn't taste or smell the lemon. She couldn't taste or smell much of anything right now. "I shouldn't have had that third glass of wine. I didn't drink all of it but it put me over the top. Usually one's my limit."

"That's a good limit."

"Scrooge was hopeless before Jacob Marley and the three Christmas spirits showed up. No one would have believed he could be happy, generous—a changed man. Yet by Christmas morning, he was. It's a story of hope, isn't it?"

Logan's hazel eyes narrowed on her as he set his mug

back on the table. "What do you want to change about who you are, Clare?"

His question took her by surprise. She covered for herself by drinking more of the tea. She could taste the lemon now, or at least convinced herself she could.

"I know every delaying tactic in the book," Logan said.

"You mean like changing the subject instead of answering which of Scrooge's ghosts got to you?"

He sighed. "The Ghost of Christmas Past. I had a nightmare about him when I was here over the weekend."

"A bad nightmare?"

He picked up his mug again and drank more of his tea. "A hell of a nightmare."

"Do you think it was because you'd just moved your grandmother into assisted living?" Clare asked. "This is the only home she's ever known. Even if she was ready to move, your subconscious could have had a field day with you."

His mouth curved in the slightest of smiles. "Are you assuming the Ghost of Christmas Past showed me what a bastard I am?"

"That's not what I meant," Clare said, steady.

"I know it wasn't. Sorry. It was a disturbing nightmare. I guess most nightmares are or they wouldn't be nightmares. I'd never slept in this house alone. I stayed in my father's old room. It hasn't changed much since he was a kid. It's not a shrine to his childhood—my grandparents just didn't see the need to spend money redecorating."

"I admire that kind of frugality."

"They weren't cheap. If they could manage without buying something new, they generally did. It was a mind-set with them as a couple at work more than necessity. Gran has enough to live on and she knows my father, sister and I would help out if she was in need."

Clare pictured the elderly woman in her chair in her new apartment. "She strikes me as highly independent."

"She is, and that sense of independence helped her to understand that living here on her own wasn't the best choice for her." Logan abandoned his tea, but he seemed to enjoy talking about his grandmother. "She's a saver by nature, but I think she wants to leave as much to us and her favorite charities as she can rather than spend it on herself."

"That's sweet," Clare said. "Provided she's not denying herself something she needs or really wants."

"I don't think she is. I hope not, anyway."

"Did the Ghost of Christmas Past remind you of your happy times with your grandparents?"

"It did not. At first I didn't remember the details,

but on my drive to Boston…" He cleared his throat. "I dreamed about a fire my grandfather tackled in his days as a firefighter. It was early Christmas morning. We were here. I was eleven. I was the only one up— sneaking into my Christmas stocking—when he left. Gran came downstairs, and she made me hot chocolate while we waited."

"Did everything turn out all right?" Clare asked softly.

"A Christmas tree caught on fire. The firefighters saved the family—the parents and three small children. The mother was badly burned. I overheard him tell Gran. I remember feeling the overwhelming desire to be able to help. To know something, to have the strength…" He trailed off, staring at his tea. "I wanted to make a difference the way my grandfather had that night."

"And your nightmare reminded you of that."

"In a hell of an unpleasant way, yes. Now." Logan leaned over the table toward her. "I told you about my visit from the Ghost of Christmas Past, who clearly wants me not to be a self-absorbed jerk. What would your Ghost of Christmas Past want you to change about yourself?"

That I can fall in love again, she thought immediately. But she didn't—couldn't—say that aloud. Instead she smiled, hoping to change the tone of the conversation. "What would I change about myself? Hmm. I think I'd change liking red wine as much as I do, since it means I'm not as sharp and clear-eyed as you are right now, which puts me at a distinct disadvantage."

"I'm not talking about that kind of change. If Scrooge's ghosts visited you, where would they take you? What kind of change would they be trying to bring forth in you?"

"Are you saying I'm an Ebenezer Scrooge?"

"I'm making conversation."

"It's an intense conversation if we're to be serious." She thought a moment, the effects of her evening out easing. "All right. I think the Ghost of Christmas Past would remind me of a time when I was more adventurous and less fearful of bad things happening."

Logan settled back in his chair, studying her. "What would a more adventurous Clare Morgan look like?"

"Well, I suppose sleeping in the nude on rough sheets for a start."

He pushed back his chair. "Clare."

"I did say that, didn't I? Saying such things is adventurous, isn't it?"

"Provocative depending on who you're saying them to."

Her eyelids suddenly felt heavy, but she didn't feel sleepy. To the contrary. "And who would that be?" she asked finally.

"A man engaging in a late-night talk with a woman recovering from a bit too much wine." He tapped the rim of his mug with one finger. "I'm also a man struggling not to picture said woman sleeping in the nude on rough sheets."

"I see."

"I'm not sure you do see."

"I'll think of something else adventurous." She ignored the heat surging through her. "I'm not white-water kayaking or ocean kayaking. That's *too* adventurous. Kayaking in a quiet lake would be adventurous enough for me. I could hike up Mount Washington. Brandon Sloan is getting into adventure travel with Dylan McCaffrey. Maggie said they want to do a trip to Newfoundland. *That* would be an adventure."

"What about emotional adventures?"

"You mean like—what?"

"Opening yourself up to people. Allowing yourself to be vulnerable." He spoke matter-of-factly, but his tone didn't match his steady gaze. "Trusting someone with your deepest hopes and dreams. Falling in love. I'm speaking generally. I'm not saying any of those things would be adventures for you."

"Easier to go white-water kayaking, maybe," she said with a lightness she didn't feel.

He smiled. "Maybe."

"I'll give it some thought, how's that? And you, Logan? Would Scrooge's ghosts want to stop you from becoming a self-absorbed jerk or reform you because you already are one?" She didn't hear an edge in her voice—didn't mean for there to be one—but saw him wince, as if she'd smacked him on the cheek. "Oh, no. I went too far. I was trying to be funny and it totally didn't work. It's hard when I'm…my head…" She yawned, covering her mouth with one hand, then slumped in her chair. "I'm sorry if I offended you."

"I probably have a thinner skin than I should about people thinking I'm an arrogant, self-absorbed jerk," he said, getting to his feet. "Maybe that's because sometimes I am a self-absorbed, arrogant jerk. But that's not what Scrooge's ghosts would want me to get out of their visits. I don't think so, anyway."

"What would they want?"

"I think they'd want me to embrace the possibility of love—to believe and live as if it's as important as work, duty, responsibility and all sorts of other positives." He gazed down at her for a moment. "I think they'd want that for you, too. More so than white-water kayaking."

Clare jumped up from the table. "Have you had wine, too?"

"A beer with Brandon Sloan."

She tried to laugh. "There you go."

"You're not comfortable with the direction of this conversation, are you, Clare?"

"I facilitate deep conversations in book clubs. Being part of one—" She swept up her tea mug. "Most of the time I talk to Owen."

"Owen's deep for a six-year-old." Logan smiled and picked up his own mug. "You're done in. I'll show you to your room."

"You can just tell me—"

"It's okay, Clare. I'm not going to seduce a woman who's had wine and chamomile tea."

"Oh."

He laughed. "You sound disappointed. That's the merlot talking."

"I said 'oh' because I don't know what else to say. I feel like I'm six steps behind what's going on here."

"I have you at a disadvantage."

"Yes, you do. I'm lucky you're—what did you say? Obedient and dutiful?"

He made a face. "Me and the family dog."

"Responsible. Not obedient. Sorry. You're also an achiever. Anything in particular you're trying to achieve right now?"

"Other than getting you to bed, you mean?"

Her breath caught in her throat. He laughed again, nodding toward the hall. "You can sleep in my father's old room. The other two bedrooms are in a state of disarray with the move, the book sorting and the decorating."

"Where will you sleep?"

"On the couch. It's not a problem. I'm used to sleeping when and where I can." He stood back, letting her go ahead of him up the stairs. "I'll catch you if you fall."

"Thanks," she said. "I'd have been more prepared but I didn't know I'd be going out with Maggie tonight."

She mounted the stairs, steadier if also more tired. He slipped an arm around her waist and steered her down the hall to the bedroom. He kissed her on the cheek. "I hope no ghosts of any kind visit you tonight," he whispered, a touch of humor in his voice.

Once the door shut, Clare let out a cathartic breath. She couldn't expect herself to keep up with the dynamics between her and Logan tonight. She needed to get some sleep, wake up and pretend they hadn't talked about ghosts and adventures and love and whatever else they'd talked about. Because she *couldn't* let herself be attracted to him. She was the shiny object he couldn't have. Once he had her, he would be on to the next shiny object. She had to think about protecting herself.

She stripped off her clothes and left them in a heap on the floor beside one of the twin beds.

"I put out a fresh toothbrush on the sink," Logan said

through the door. "Gran had a half-dozen brand-new toothbrushes in a drawer."

"Thank you." Clare grabbed a quilt off the end of the bed and wrapped it around her, as if he could see her through the door. "I could learn a few things from your grandmother."

"We all could. Was I right about the sheets?"

"I haven't gotten that far yet."

She could almost see his smile. "Good night, Clare."

She waited a full minute before she lowered the quilt and climbed into the bed. She was so tired, so giddy, that she laughed out loud when her skin touched the sheets. Logan hadn't exaggerated. The sheets were pure sandpaper, and yet somehow perfect.

When she awoke, Clare had a dry mouth and a vague, troubling sense she'd made a fool out of herself last night. She sat up, yawning, realizing she remembered everything about tea with Logan. She hadn't been drunk, and she didn't have a hangover. She just was out of her comfort zone.

Sunlight streamed in through the bedroom window. She hadn't thought to pull the shades.

She glanced at the bedside clock and moaned. *Nine* o'clock?

Nine?

She couldn't remember the last time she'd slept this late. She wasn't sure she ever *had* slept this late. Why hadn't the sunshine awakened her?

Because it was winter, she supposed, and the sun rose later—and because she'd wormed her way deep under the covers in her sleep.

She'd forgotten she wasn't wearing any clothes.

Time to make her excuses and get herself home. If Owen wasn't ready to leave his friends, she'd come back for him.

She put on last night's clothes, made the bed and went down the hall to the bathroom. Logan's shaving gear was in a black case on a shelf next to the sink. It struck her as incredibly intimate, a tangible reminder that he was a real, live man and not some fantasy she'd created.

Her reflection showed a real, live woman with smeared mascara and bad hair.

After she washed up, she found a brush in a drawer and did her best with her hair, but it was a lost cause. She wasn't being hard on herself. She was looking in the mirror and assessing the situation with clarity and objectivity. She dug around in more drawers and found a covered rubber band.

Perfect.

She pulled her hair into a loose ponytail. It would have to do.

When she got downstairs, Logan had strings of lights untangled and neatly laid out on the living room floor. "These are the indoor lights," he said. "We probably won't need all of them."

"All of them for what?"

He looked up from his work. "I thought we could collect Owen and go out to the farm and cut a Christmas tree." He smiled. "After you've had coffee and breakfast."

"Thank you. Good morning. I overslept."

"Excellent. And good morning to you."

She wasn't used to waking up to a man in the house. "I can get breakfast at home."

"As you wish, but I can manage coffee, cereal and banana here if that suits you."

"It does, thanks. Sorry I missed the untangling of the lights."

"I'm surprised you didn't hear me cursing. Gran was organized about everything except putting away the Christmas lights, which makes me think someone else did it. Probably not my grandfather, since he was just as organized. I suspect my father had a hand in it."

"When was the last Christmas you spent here?"

"Long time."

It wasn't a question he wanted to answer, obviously. One of those can-of-worms questions that Clare knew better than to stumble into and yet often did. She felt guilty for asking, but he changed the subject as they went into the kitchen, chatting amiably about the sunshine and perfect conditions to cut a Christmas tree.

"Are you up for cutting a tree?" he asked as he made coffee.

She got out the cereal and banana. "Absolutely."

NINE

>‹‹

*... There is nothing in the world so irresistibly
contagious as laughter and good humour.*

—Charles Dickens, *A Christmas Carol*

THE FARRELL FAMILY FARM BORDERED THE
Quabbin watershed on the outskirts of Knights Bridge.
Logan hadn't been out here in several years. The old
stone walls and sugar maples made him think of bygone
times. His life in Boston seemed not only far away but
in a different century. He could see generations of Farrells here, working the land, eking a subsistence exis-
tence out of the rocky soil and tough conditions. They
hadn't run a commercial farm. They'd farmed to live.
They'd had pigs, chickens, a cow, a garden.

Logan didn't romanticize that life. His grandfather had inherited the farm upon his father's death but by then he had a home in town and was content as the fire chief. He hadn't wanted to sell the place. Eventually he and Daisy had decided to adopt a sustainable forestry plan to cut down on property taxes. Upon Tom Farrell's death, the farm had gone to Logan's father. No one had been more surprised than Logan when his parents had announced their plans to renovate the house and retire here.

White pine, red oak and black walnut dominated the trees that were technically part of the forestry plan for the property, but his grandparents had also planted a field of balsam firs intended for Christmas trees. They were in a field above the old farmhouse, which was now empty as Logan's parents prepared for their retirement.

Logan unlocked the shed and got a bow saw off the nail where it had hung for decades. No chain saw for him. He didn't have a lot of experience with chain saws, but he also wanted to create an old-fashioned experience for Clare and her son.

"I've never cut down a Christmas tree before," Owen said excitedly as Logan fell in next to him and his mother.

"You can help pick it out, too," Logan said. "Have you and your mother put up your tree yet?"

The boy shook his head. "We don't have room for a tree where we live."

Logan was familiar with the apartment Clare was renting at the old sawmill, and it *was* small. Fitting a tree in there would take ingenuity, creativity and determination—not to mention hard work given the steep, narrow stairs up from the ground floor.

"We could always do a tabletop tree," Clare said.

Owen contemplated that option with the seriousness of a six-year-old. "Will Santa know a kid lives there? Grandma and Grandpa had a little tree on their table last year. Santa didn't come to their house."

Logan noticed Clare bite back a smile but he was sure Owen didn't know. "Santa will know. He knew Grandma and Grandpa were older, didn't he?" She hung back with Logan as Owen shot ahead of them, navigating the shoveled walk from the shed with ease. "We have fun with the notion of Santa Claus."

"I do, too," Logan said. "Santa doesn't have creepy ghosts who drag your ass out of bed in the middle of the night."

Clare laughed. "I didn't encounter any ghosts last night."

It was going to kill him, that laugh of hers, Logan thought. It was a window to her heart, no question—the place where she wasn't fretting, planning or remembering, just enjoying the moment. He was glad being here with him was bringing that out in her, even if cutting a

Christmas tree was going to involve getting snow in his face. He saw that now, as they approached a row of six-foot-tall spruce trees, their branches drooping with snow.

"I don't remember snow on the branches when I cut trees with my grandfather," he said.

Clare looked amused. "The wind probably blew it off."

"Or my grandfather did some prep work. I didn't think of it. You up to this, Clare?"

"The ultimate challenge," she said. "Shaking snow off a Christmas tree."

"I want *this* tree," Owen said, standing in front of a tall fir that had to have the most snow on it of any in the field.

Logan tucked the saw into the snow next to another tree. He pointed at it. "Do not touch the saw, Owen. Understood?"

He nodded solemnly. "But I want to help," he said.

"You can help, but you have to do what I say. The saw has a very sharp blade. We don't want to get cut."

No argument from Owen. Clare looked noticeably paler, but she was naturally pale and they were surrounded by white snow. She'd rallied after her evening with the Knights Bridge women. A good night's sleep, All-Bran and banana, coffee and a shower had returned her to normal. Sawing down a Christmas tree with her son might set her back, but Logan wasn't worried.

"Have you ever cut your own Christmas tree?" he asked her.

She shook her head. "No, never. It'll be fun."

"Except for the snow in our faces," Logan said, grinning.

"That I can handle."

"We can have hot chocolate afterward to warm up."

Owen turned around, knee-deep in snow, and waved to them. He was obviously eager to get started. "Can I use the saw?"

Clare gulped in a breath. "No, Owen, you're too young."

"I can let him hold it, take a few swipes," Logan said. "I'll do the real sawing."

"You've done this before?" she asked him.

"I have, indeed."

"Alone?"

"You mean without a local guy helping? No, I've never cut down a tree on my own. I always had my grandfather with me. I don't blame you if you'd be more comfortable if I called Brandon Sloan to supervise, but I think we can handle the job."

"We don't need to call Brandon," she said.

"Good, because if I screw this up, I don't want a Sloan as a witness."

She gave a small laugh. "You don't want to be the city-slicker doctor who's all thumbs with a saw."

She had her game face on, but Logan could see she was concerned about her son getting into a mess. Logan wasn't as experienced with saws as locals like the Sloans, but he wasn't entirely all thumbs. He suspected she knew it—but he also had nothing to prove. Cutting down a six-foot Christmas balsam fir didn't exceed his limits, whether he was using a handsaw or a chain saw.

Owen dived into his chosen tree, shaking the snow off, giggling when it blew in his face and then in his mother's and Logan's faces. Logan got snow down his back, too. Into the fun, Owen made a snowball and threw it at his mother, hitting her in the stomach. She laughed and made a show of going after him with a snowball of her own.

"Logan, help me," Owen yelled, squealing with delight. "Help me, Logan! Save me from Mom!"

Logan caught Clare around the middle, but she was fast and nailed him in the chest with the snowball. It went down his front. Her eyes widened. "Uh-oh. I meant to get your jacket."

"Ah, that's cold." He held on to her. "Really cold."

"Good one, Mom," Owen said. "It's only snow, Logan."

"What are you going to do with me?" she asked in a low voice.

"I'll save my revenge for when you least expect it."

Logan winked, then released her.

Their little snowball fight, combined with getting as much snow as possible off the tree branches, kept them moving and therefore warm. He got the saw and explained its function to Owen. In short order, they had the tree cut. It was a good size and a classic shape that was perfect for his grandparents' house. He, Owen and Clare pitched in together to drag it through the snow to the driveway. He'd thrown rope and bungee cords into his car before leaving the house. By the time they got the tree tied onto the roof rack, Owen was bored and starting to shiver.

"What do you say we go back to my grandmother's house for lunch?"

The boy clapped his mitten-covered hands together. "Yay!"

"Are you sure?" Clare asked. "We don't want to overstay our welcome."

"Not possible. And who's to say I'm not bribing you with food so you'll help set up the tree? It'll have to dry out before we can string lights and decorate." Logan nodded back toward the Christmas-tree fields. "We'll come back for your tabletop tree."

"Does this mean you've put aside your zest for revenge?"

He grinned. "Not a chance."

When they arrived in the village, Logan parked on the street because a car was already in the driveway. Logan didn't recognize it. "Do you know whose car it is?" he asked Clare.

"I think it's Audrey Frost's car."

"Gran's yoga partner," he said. "Randy's mother."

"She still has her own car. Why would she be here? I hope nothing's happened."

"Let's find out."

Clare's mind had obviously gone to negative possibilities, but Logan had learned in his work to take one thing at a time. Owen hopped out of the car, and he and Clare followed him onto the porch and in through the front door.

They found his grandmother and Audrey Frost in the kitchen, baking. "Daisy had an urge for molasses cookies," Audrey said. "Olivia and Jess stopped in for a visit and mentioned Maggie brought molasses cookies to their little soiree last night. You know how it is, especially this time of year. Once you start thinking about molasses cookies, you can't stop until you have a couple of them warm out of the oven—with a tall glass of cold milk."

Daisy had a worn-looking recipe card on the counter next to her mixing bowl. "Molasses cookies were Tom's favorite."

"It's okay for us to be here," Audrey said. "Rivendell isn't a prison. We have to sign out so they know where we are. We lost Grace Webster last spring and had to launch a search party. Quote-unquote lost her. She borrowed my car and went off on her own. All's well that ends well, right, Daisy?"

Her older friend sniffed. "Grace scared the daylights out of half the town, but she had her reasons."

"A secret lover from the past," Audrey whispered to Clare.

Daisy waved a hand. "It's not a secret anymore. Oh, my. Smell those molasses cookies."

"Gran," Logan said, "how long has that jar of molasses been on that shelf?"

"I don't know. Molasses doesn't go bad."

He examined the jar. No mold, no bad smell. The "use by" date was blocked by dried molasses. As far as he knew, his grandmother only used it for baked beans and cookies. At least it was a small jar. She couldn't do much baking without replacing it. It was too late, anyway—a batch of cookies was already in the oven.

By his mother's wise decree, Owen was allowed only one sweet. He chose warm cookies out of the oven and decided to save hot chocolate for another day. When Audrey pulled a tray of plump, ginger-colored cookies out of the oven, Logan knew he wouldn't resist, either. She unloaded the cookies onto a cooling rack and set the tray on top of the stove for Daisy to spoon on the next batch.

Clare picked up a steaming cookie. It was clearly hotter than she'd expected. It broke in half, but she caught it before it could fall to the floor. "This is so good," she said, popping a chunk of cookie in her mouth. "Hot but good."

Her fight with the hot cookie nearly undid Logan. Tongue, lips, long, graceful fingers, the way her breasts moved when she jumped. He breathed slowly, but when he reached for a cookie, he noticed Audrey Frost giving him the evil eye. Damned if she didn't look like her son. He grinned at her. "Can't resist Christmas sweets," he said, all innocence.

She pointed a bony finger at him. "I know what you're up to, Logan Farrell."

"You're sharp as a tack," he said.

He noticed his grandmother leaning into the counter, her breathing steady but raspy as she spooned the last of the cookie dough onto the tray. He edged over to her. "Let me put the tray in the oven and get the dishes," he said.

"I made a big mess. I've never been a neat cook."

"Have a seat, Gran. Do you want milk or tea with your cookies?"

She beamed. "Tea would be wonderful."

"Allow me," Clare said.

She grabbed the kettle and made tea while Audrey sat at the table opposite her friend. Logan knew both women were more tired after their cookie-baking adventure than they wanted to admit. He felt a bruise on his knee from his tree-cutting, but it was worth it to have a fresh, healthy balsam fir to put up in the front room one last time. He'd also enjoyed spending time with Clare and little Owen.

The boy regaled the two older women with his version of their morning, including the snowball fight. "Mom got snow down Logan's front," he said.

Both women raised their eyebrows, almost simultaneously. "Did she?" Audrey said. "Well, good for her."

"If I'd been aiming, I never would have managed," Clare said with a laugh.

"Nice to come back from romping in the snow to cookies fresh out of the oven." Logan grabbed one off the rack. "Gran, when's the last time you made these?"

"It's been several years. I used to make them every Christmas when you and your sister were little. Then your grandfather and I cut back on sweets." She shrugged expansively. "Things change."

"I hate to cook," Audrey said. "I've always hated it, but we had to eat. My late husband helped with meals, but he didn't like cooking, either. That's one of the best things about moving into assisted living. I don't have to cook."

"The food is excellent," Daisy said.

Audrey grinned. "I gained three pounds my first month there. My doctor had a fit."

Clare filled a teapot and got out cups and saucers. She filled a small white-china pitcher with milk. Daisy pointed out where Clare could find Christmas napkins she'd saved in a drawer in the dining room. Logan opted out of tea, content to watch Clare with her son and the two elderly women enjoy themselves. Clare was comfortable around people, more so than she might realize.

After their cookies and tea, Audrey yawned, visibly tired, and got stiffly to her feet. "I sat up late watching a Bruins game. I never understood ice hockey that well, but Dylan gave me a few pointers."

"You go on," Daisy said. "Logan can run me back to my place when I'm ready. Can't you, Logan?"

"Of course, Gran."

He wrapped up cookies for Audrey to take back with her. He'd give Clare and Owen some, too. No way was he eating four dozen molasses cookies on his own. After Audrey left, Clare turned the faucet on in the sink. "I'll clean up the dishes and then head back—unless you want me to clear out now."

"I want you to stay," Daisy said, an authority coming into her voice that reminded Logan this was her house. "Please," she added.

"I'd be happy to."

Daisy put a thin arm over Owen's shoulders. "There's a chest of drawers in the dining room. The bottom drawer has kids' stuff in it. I can't remember what all is in there. Help yourself."

Owen's eyes lit up. He didn't need to be told twice and ran into the dining room.

Daisy reached for her walker. "I'd like to see the candle you found." She took in a breath, getting her second wind. "There's a story that goes with it."

A Recipe for Molasses Cookies

—— ➤ ⟵ ——

¾ cup butter (preferably unsalted)
1 cup sugar
¼ cup molasses
1 egg
2 cups all-purpose flour
2 teaspoons baking soda
½ teaspoon cloves
½ teaspoon ginger
½ teaspoon cinnamon
½ teaspoon salt (optional)

Preheat oven to 375°F. Melt butter. Combine sugar, molasses and egg. Add melted butter and mix well. Combine remaining ingredients. Add to butter mixture and blend together. Chill the dough. Once chilled, form into small balls (about walnut size) and roll in sugar. Place on cookie sheet and bake for 8 to 10 minutes.

TEN

>←←

The Phantom slowly, gravely, silently approached...
It was shrouded in a deep black garment...nothing
of it visible save one outstretched hand.

—CHARLES DICKENS, *A CHRISTMAS CAROL*

WHATEVER THE STORY THAT WENT WITH
the candle, Daisy Farrell was keeping it to herself.
Whether she wasn't ready to tell it or never would, Clare
couldn't say. She only knew that seeing Daisy hold the
old, half-melted candle in her hands, her eyes filling
with tears, had been enough to set her back on her heels.

Clare stood on the front walk to her apartment and
watched the water flow over the dam. She needed the
sounds, the cold—the fresh air.

"Mom, are you crying?" Owen asked, holding her hand.

"A little."

"It's okay to cry. Did you hurt yourself?"

She shook her head. "Logan's grandmother found something from a long time ago and it brought tears to my eyes." She forced a smile. "It wasn't sad. It was touching. Sort of sad and happy at the same time."

"I know," Owen said, solemn.

She laughed, then crouched next to him. She pointed across the stream to the opposite bank. "Do you see the tracks in the snow?"

He dropped her hand and jumped up. "I do!"

"What kind of animal do you think the tracks belong to?"

"White-tail deer, probably."

"Let's go upstairs and see if we can spot them from our window. We can use the binoculars and get a closer look."

"I think there should be a bridge over the brook, don't you, Mom?"

"That would be great," she said. "Our very own footbridge."

"Yeah," he said. "No cars allowed."

Clare laughed. "Right, no cars allowed."

They continued their conversation about a potential

bridge and the animal tracks as they headed upstairs. By the time they reached their warm apartment, any tears had vanished. Daisy's expression when she'd held the candle had affected Clare more than she'd have ever expected.

Logan had sent them off with molasses cookies. Once Owen settled himself at the window with the binoculars, Clare put the cookies into a basket in the kitchen. The past day crushed in on her, this new life of hers in small-town Knights Bridge not as slow-paced and easy-going as she'd expected. It was challenging her on every level—except professionally, she thought. She had no trouble handling her duties as library director, and was filled with excitement and ideas.

"But there it is, isn't it?"

She spoke aloud in her tiny, empty kitchen. Her personal life was suddenly filling her with excitement and ideas, too, but she wasn't as comfortable with them as the ones in her professional life, where she was more confident. Decorating for Christmas with Logan, cutting down a balsam fir, seeing him interact with his grandmother—spending the night in the same house with him—were new and unfamiliar experiences, stirring up emotions and urges she'd long left behind.

"Mom!"

She ran into the living room. "What is it, Owen?"

He was pointing outside. She thought he must have spotted an animal—a deer or a wild turkey, even a rabbit. "Look," he said. "It's Logan."

"Logan Farrell?"

Owen nodded, excited. "And he has a *Christmas tree*."

Clare didn't know what to think. The man was tireless, relentless. Having all that energy focused on her, even for a day, was unbelievable—and more dangerous and intoxicating than a few glasses of wine, for sure.

She went downstairs and opened the door for him. "Owen spotted you," she said. "We saw tracks in the snow—he was looking for wild animals."

He grinned, his face all angles in the evening shadows. "Do I fit the bill or was he expecting a wolf or a fox?"

"Wild turkeys and deer, maybe."

"Well, I hope he didn't mistake me for a turkey."

Clare laughed, then stood back. "Won't you come in?"

"I'll take this upstairs." He held up a small but healthy-looking balsam fir. "It's the runt of the litter—the top part of a crooked tree. I found it on the edge of the field where we cut the one for Gran's house."

"It's perfect."

"It can be your Charlie Brown Christmas tree. Do you have any decorations?"

"A few," she said.

"You can grab extras from Gran's boxes. We won't

need half of them for the tree at her house. Decorations are secondary. I want to string lights so they can be seen from outside."

"She's going to help you decorate?"

"By 'we' I mean you and I."

He didn't give Clare a chance to answer, instead heading past her up the stairs with the tree. It was too big for a tabletop but it was small enough that she wasn't worried about finding a place for it in the living room.

Still a little taken aback, she followed him up the stairs.

Owen squealed in excitement both at having Logan there and at the sight of the Christmas tree. "Our own Christmas tree," he said in amazement, as if he'd never had one before.

"I have a stand in the car, if you need one," Logan said, turning to Clare as he leaned the tree against the wall.

"I do need one," she said. "Thank you."

He went back out for the stand. She sank onto the couch, smelling the evergreen, regaining her composure.

Owen fingered a branch. "Where should we put it?"

"I thought maybe in front of the window."

"No one will see it," he said.

"That's because we live in the country. But we'll see it, and Mr. and Mrs. Frost will see it—and the animals in the forest will see it."

That perked him up. "Animals like Christmas, too, don't they, Mom?"

"I'm sure they'll appreciate a Christmas tree twinkling in the window."

Logan returned with the stand. "I dried off the tree as much as possible, but you'll want to give it a day or two before you decorate."

He enlisted Owen's help and got the little tree set up in front of the window. Clare watched them, Logan patiently instructing Owen, Owen listening carefully. *Don't let yourself get attached*, she told herself. More important, she couldn't let Owen get attached. Logan was spending time in Knights Bridge because helping his grandmother move had fallen to him, and he'd agreed to decorate her house. After that, he had no reason to stay. Given the emotions of his grandmother's situation, it was no wonder he had latched onto a widow and her young son.

But as they finished setting up the tree, Clare found herself inviting Logan to stay for dinner. "It won't be fancy—whatever I have in the freezer."

"What if I told you Maggie Sloan brought over a pot of her homemade chili as I was leaving to take Gran back to her apartment?"

"Maggie's chili is legendary."

"So I hear. I just happened to put the pot in my backseat and strap it in as I headed out." He slung an arm over her shoulders. "Chili for dinner, and then tomorrow you and Owen can help get the tree we cut this morning into a stand. I think it'll take all three of us, don't you, Owen?"

"Yeah," he said, already heading for the door. "I can help carry the chili."

As if Logan needed help, but he smiled. "There's salad and corn bread, too." He winked at Clare. "We owe Maggie. She loves to cook and help out, but maybe between now and Christmas we could have her boys for an overnight at my grandmother's house. Give her and Brandon a chance for a date night."

"I'm sure they'd like that," Clare said, keeping her tone neutral.

"How would you like it?" he asked, his gaze settling on her.

"I'd love to do something for Brandon and Maggie. The boys would be able to spread out at Daisy's house. It gets cramped fast here, but I'm sure they'd manage to find something to do. And you'd be there?"

"I'd be there." He nodded toward the kitchen. "Let's see how good Maggie's chili is."

Clare didn't know which she liked best—the chili, the salad or the corn bread. After her intense day, she appreciated the substantial, simple meal and not having to cook. As she cleaned up in the kitchen and Owen showed Logan his latest Lego project, she texted Maggie to convey her thanks.

Maggie replied immediately. Is our ER doc still there?

Yes.

Say the word, and I'll spirit Owen away.

Clare felt blood rush to her face, but she smiled as she typed. Maggie!

Consider me your new best friend.

The chili is amazing.

Clare returned to the living room. Owen had gone to his room to play and Logan was sitting on the rug in front of the couch. "I can hear the water running over the dam," he said. "Must be soothing in warm weather when you can open the windows."

"I think it will be. I keep a close eye on Owen with the brook and dam right there." Clare sat on the couch, her left knee inches from Logan's shoulder. "There are cookies if you want one, but I couldn't eat another bite. The corn bread was like a dessert."

"Maggie's good at what she does." He leaned back against the seat cushion next to her. "If I hadn't already had a couple of the cookies, I'd be into your stash now. Tramping through snow, sawing, dragging Christmas trees, loading them onto the car—that'll earn you a few extra goodies."

"You're used to a frenetic pace, aren't you?"

"Not every day is hectic. A lot of them are, though." He looked up at her. "What about you? Are you getting your feet under you at the library?"

"It took a while just not to get lost. I can see why people think the building is haunted."

"More ghosts. Just what I need."

"Are you going back to Boston tonight, or are you spending the night at your grandmother's house?"

"Spending the night. We have trees to decorate."

"Here?" Owen asked as he shot into the living room.

"Not here," Logan said. "At my grandmother's house."

"I like it there."

"Good. I hope your mom will let you help decorate the big tree we cut."

Owen tugged on her hand. "Can I, Mom?"

"Of course," she said.

He dragged Logan back into his room to show him

another toy. Clare collapsed against the back of the couch and blew out a breath at the ceiling, getting herself under control. She needed to tread carefully. She couldn't let Owen get too close to Logan and then have Logan disappear. She needed to protect her son from disappointment.

Logan came back out to the living room while Owen went into the bathroom to wash up. It was getting close to his bedtime. "What's on your mind?" Logan asked as he sat next to Clare on the couch.

"What makes you think something's on my mind?"

"Years of training and experience in the ER. I've developed a sixth sense for when people are keeping something from me that I need to know versus something I don't need to know but they still want to withhold. I'm guessing yours is the former."

"I don't need stitches or a cast."

"I see that."

"Owen is becoming attached to you," she said, blurting it out before she could stop herself.

Logan was silent for a moment. "From my point of view, that's a positive," he said finally.

"From my point of view, it's an unknown. I'm the only parent Owen has. I've been careful about…" She considered her next words before she continued. "I've been careful about men in my life."

"I have roots in Knights Bridge. I'm not going any-where. Owen's getting attached to Brandon Sloan, too."

"If you're implying he's missed out because he never knew his father—that I haven't done enough—" Clare stopped herself, horrified at how blunt she was being with him. No filters. He seemed capable of hearing any-thing she had to say. She bit down on her lip, forcing herself to think. "I haven't done this in a long time," she added, her voice just above a whisper.

"You've experienced how unfair and unpredictable life can be, and you want to protect your son from that as much as possible. And yourself."

"Maybe."

"No *maybe*. You turned pale when you mentioned the brook. How many times have you had Owen fall-ing into it in your mind?"

"Not as many as you might think but more than I'd like. I used to jump into things without looking, with-out thinking—like you do."

"Like I do, huh?"

"I saw it today. You grabbed that bow saw without hesitating. It never occurred to you that you might not be able to handle cutting down a Christmas tree."

He settled back against the couch. "As it turned out, I was right."

Clare couldn't help but smile. "You could have been

wrong, but that's not my point. It's easy to dive in without looking when it's just you. I remember what that was like. There are things that come up all the time for me now and I think…I could do that."

"But you stop yourself," he said.

"Sometimes. Not always. I'm a single mother with a six-year-old son who never knew his father. I can't not be that for five minutes. But it's not a burden. That's what I'm trying to say."

Logan put an arm around her and pulled her toward him. "Clare," he said. "Clare, Clare. I see you as brave and kind and intelligent, as a woman who loves her son. I don't see you as weak. Not for a second."

"Thank you."

"I know you want to protect him. I do, too. But does protecting him mean I should walk out of here right now and not ask you to come by tomorrow to help me decorate that gigantic tree that's on my grandmother's front porch?"

"Owen's counting on helping you decorate," she said.

"And you?"

"I'm counting on it, too."

He took curls that had strayed into her face between two of his fingers and tucked them behind her ear. He kissed her softly on the lips. "I do things fast," he said, kissing her again, as if to confirm his words. "I know that about myself. If I'm going too fast for you, I can slow down."

"You're not going too fast," she whispered.

"Good, because I already have slowed down." He sat up straight. "If it was up to me right now, I'd be spending the night on your sofa bed instead of back at Gran's with the ghosts."

"Have I mentioned the six-year-old in the bathroom brushing his teeth?"

"He's already told me I can sleep here."

"He wasn't thinking about where," Clare said.

"Actually, he told me I could sleep in his room with him."

"You'll be better off with the ghosts. Owen's a wiggle worm."

Logan smiled. "Does he remind you of his father?"

"He does, definitely," Clare said without hesitation. "Stephen was younger than I am now when he died. It took a long time to accept his death—that he wouldn't see Owen grow up, that Owen would never know his father. I'm the same person I was when Stephen and I married but at the same time I'm not. I don't take life for granted the way I once did. I try to remember that every day is a gift."

"A good thing to remember this time of year."

"Does your work affect you at all?"

"I can go too far in the opposite direction and live only for today. Take risks because—well, what the hell, right? You can obey all the rules, do everything right and a house falls on your head. I see it if not every day, a lot."

"And how often do you think about it?"

He grinned. "Only just now."

"Because you've got my sofa bed on your mind."

"Would it hold two people?"

"I think so. It's never had to."

"Now there's a thought," he said in a rough, sexy voice as the bathroom door creaked and Owen came into the living room, wanting Logan to read him a book.

"You bet, my friend. Pick one out. If it's too long, I'll skip parts."

Owen giggled, and Clare gave up the couch to the two of them and *How the Grinch Stole Christmas*. Logan smiled at her as she went over to her little Christmas tree. She knew he'd gotten her point. She was attracted to him, and she wanted to go further—but she wasn't a one-night stand. She wasn't going to amuse him while he dealt with his aging grandmother and her old house in small, out-of-the-way Knights Bridge.

But as Clare checked the water in the tree stand, she could still feel his lips on hers, the aftereffects of their kiss enough to make her want more. If not for her son,

she wondered if she'd be another of Logan Farrell's conquests right now, and if that would be so bad.

Not an appropriate thought while he was reading a
Christmas book to her son.

And who was she to say Logan had "conquests"?

She glanced back at him. He was confident, smart,
cocky and successful, and by his own admission, he did
things fast.

Old-fashioned word it might be, but it made the point.

He'd had conquests.

ELEVEN

➤←

"There are many things from which I might have
derived good, by which I have not profited..."

–Charles Dickens, *A Christmas Carol*

LOGAN DID DO THINGS FAST. HE HADN'T EX-
aggerated when he'd told Clare. He'd been truthful, if
not fully open and candid about what was on his mind.
He'd always known he would fall in love quickly when
the time came—when the woman he was meant to be
with walked into his life.

Why wouldn't he fall fast and hard, since that was
how he operated?

Turned out he was right.

He set up the tree stand in his grandmother's living

room. He'd brought in wood and lit a fire in the fireplace. The room glowed with the flames, the floor lamp and the lights he and Clare had strung on the porch. He could hear kids yelling and carrying on across the street on the skating rink on the town common. Apparently a heated hockey game was underway. He almost grabbed skates out of the back room and joined the festivities.

Even after his active day, he was restless, but it wasn't the kind of restlessness that playing hockey with fifteen-year-olds would ease.

Clare had every right and every reason not to trust his intentions with her. He had a busy, fulfilling job in Boston, and his ties to Knights Bridge, while deep, weren't ones that had ever made him contemplate living here. He wanted to fall in love and assumed he would one day, but he wasn't in any big rush.

Clare's life was the exact opposite of his life. She might be new to Knights Bridge, but she belonged here, taking its small but vibrant library into the next decades and raising her son. Her night out with Maggie Sloan and her friends was proof the locals were accepting her, welcoming her.

Logan checked the fasteners on the stand. They were in good working order.

What the hell, he thought. Might as well bring in the tree.

It would be a quick trip out to the porch. He grabbed work gloves out of the mudroom but didn't bother with his jacket. Maybe a shot of cold night air would help him regain his sense.

When he stepped onto the porch, he noticed snowflakes in the glow of the Christmas lights. The hockey game had broken up, the kids were packing up and heading home. Logan stood still, listening. He swore he heard singing. The local drunk singing on his way home?

No.

Carolers.

A cold winter night in a quiet village, and he could hear carolers.

He couldn't see them in the dark, but he thought they were across the common, near the Swift River Country Store.

They finished "Joy to the World" and started on "We Wish You a Merry Christmas."

He'd forgotten that caroling was a tradition in the village. His grandfather would join them from time to time. *He can sing like an angel*, his grandmother had told Logan. *I never could hold a tune.*

What a life his grandparents had lived here in their little town, Logan thought.

He saw the silhouette of a couple under the lights on the rink, skating arm in arm, flowing over the ice. He heard the pair laugh, and he finally recognized Dylan McCaffrey and his fiancée, Olivia Frost. Olivia, an accomplished graphic designer, had lived in Boston for several years, but she'd always wanted to move back to her hometown—at least according to Audrey, her grandmother.

Logan's throat tightened, and he pictured himself skating with Clare. Did she know how to skate? He did, but not like ex-NHL player Dylan. A multimillionaire, Dylan was making a place for himself in Knights Bridge. That he was marrying a local woman and opening businesses in town probably helped his relationship with the locals.

Of course, Dylan didn't have to live down a reputation as an arrogant, selfish Boston ER doctor who had neglected his grandmother.

Logan shivered. Damn, it was cold. All he needed was hypothermia. Some ER doctor.

The gloves kept the fir needles from pricking his hands, but they nailed him on his cheek as he maneuvered the tree through the door and into the front room. He was breathing hard by the time he propped it into the stand.

A hunk of melting snow he'd missed on one of the branches plopped off, straight down his back.

"Clare, Clare," he said. "Why aren't you here?"

Why hadn't he brought her to the chili instead of the chili to her?

He tightened the tree into the stand, ignoring more drips and splashes of melting snow. By the time he finished, he had wet hair and a wet shirt, and his face and hands—he'd had to take off the gloves—were covered in red marks from the needles. They stung and they itched.

He lay back on the rug and laughed, imagining his grandfather getting a big kick out of his only grandson's machinations with the balsam fir.

It felt good to miss his grandfather, and right. The rest of Knights Bridge missed him, too.

Logan sat up, heading to the kitchen for a well-earned beer. As he opened it, he looked at his reflection in the window above the sink. He wasn't a perfect man. He could be a better man, but he would never be a perfect one.

He was falling in love with Clare Morgan.

And he was falling in love with her fast.

An unwelcome visit from Jacob Marley roused Logan early. He didn't know if he preferred skeletal old Marley warning him to mend his ways or one of Scrooge's spirits, but he knew he wasn't going back to sleep. He took a shower, got dressed and walked across the common to Smith's. He noticed a good scratch on his right hand. Must have bloodied himself hauling in the tree last night. Next up was decorating it. If he was taking another go at the six-foot fir, he needed a good breakfast.

As he sat in a two-person booth, a few Sloans entered the restaurant.

"Want some company?" Justin asked.

Logan motioned to the cushioned bench across from him. "Have a seat."

Christopher and Eric Sloan sat at a nearby table. Their presence palpably raised the energy level in the place. Brandon joined them. Only Adam was missing—the stonemason brother, as Logan recalled.

"Looks like you had some fun," Justin said, pointing to the scratch on Logan's hand.

"I got in a fight with a balsam fir."

"Nasty bastards." Justin grinned, settling back against the booth. "Hope you cleaned your wound. Wouldn't want it to get infected."

"Good advice. Thanks."

As Logan chatted with Justin over breakfast, with a few comments from the Sloans at the next table, he wondered if his beer with Brandon had helped thaw his brothers' attitude toward him.

Heather, the youngest and the only female, joined Brandon, Christopher and Eric at their table. A fresh round of sibling teasing ensued. Logan understood that was how they communicated with each other, and Heather—dark-haired and blue-eyed like the male Sloans—gave as good as she got, clearly up to the challenge of dealing with five older brothers.

Justin added milk to his fresh coffee refill. "How long are you in town this time?" he asked Logan.

"I go back to Boston later today."

"We're working out at the McCaffrey place for a few hours today," Justin said. "We're making up for taking Wednesday afternoon for our annual Christmas party."

"I'm making eggnog from scratch," Heather interjected from her table.

"Which no one will touch," Eric added.

She rolled her eyes. "Anyone can make eggnog. Besides, I'll add bourbon. Can't go wrong."

"You can," her eldest brother said, grinning at her.

"I did do a dry run that didn't go so well," she said. "It had little threads of egg in it. Totally gross. Mom says to drain it through cheesecloth."

Christopher grimaced. "Pour the bourbon, skip the eggnog."

"That would be easier, too," Heather said. She turned to Logan. "You see how this works, Dr. Farrell? All of a sudden I only have to bring Jack Daniel's to the party."

Before Logan could comment, her brothers jumped in and pressed their case against her cooking abilities. She took their teasing in stride, giving as good as she got. Logan decided to keep quiet.

Brandon turned in his chair. "Maggie's stopping by to help Clare take the rest of Daisy's old books to the library. They won't be in the way, will they?"

Logan shook his head. "Not at all. We're decorating the tree we cut on the farm yesterday. I hadn't done that since I was a kid. My grandfather and I would go out together."

"He always let us pick out a tree," Justin said. "Good memories."

If he meant to be critical or skeptical, it didn't show in his voice. A welcome thaw, Logan thought, given their last breakfast together.

After breakfast, he walked across the common. If he were in Boston, he'd either be sleeping late or grabbing a latte at Starbucks on his way to the hospital. *Maybe* working out at his health club, but he usually hit the treadmill and weights after his shift, whatever time it ended. He had a nonstop schedule but it could feel random. Life in Knights Bridge felt more ordered—or at least more predictable. He doubted much had changed in town since his grandparents had been teenagers.

Clare had arrived with Owen when Logan got back to his grandmother's house. "Good morning," she said, rosy-cheeked from the cold weather.

Maggie pulled in behind them. "Oh, my," she said as they all entered the house. "Look at that tree. It's gorgeous just with the lights. I'll have to walk by the house when it gets dark and see the lights in the window. Do you have them on a timer, so they'll come on even when you're in Boston?"

"I don't, but it's a good idea," Logan said. "I'll set it up before I leave this afternoon."

"Can we decorate the tree now?" Owen asked.

"I can help," Maggie said. "Or I can come back later—"

"No, no, stay, please," Clare said. "You're bound to have a good eye for decorating a Christmas tree. It won't take long. Then we can grab the books. Logan, is it okay with you? Or did you decide you want to play Christmas music and decorate the tree by yourself?"

Logan grinned. "How did you guess?"

They decorated the tree in short order. He picked up Owen to let him hang decorations on the highest branches. Clare found a star for the top of the tree. Maggie was a whiz at plucking just the right balls and baubles from the boxes.

As they finished, Maggie got a call. Logan could tell instantly it wasn't anything good. He glanced at Clare, who had gone slightly pale, watching her friend. When Maggie got off the phone, she turned to them. "Brandon's uncle Pete had a bad encounter with a nail gun. Brandon says there's blood everywhere."

"Is there anything I can do?" Logan asked.

"Pete's got his hand wrapped in a towel. He won't let them call an ambulance. Says if he needs stitches, he'll drive himself to the ER."

Not an attitude with which Logan was unfamiliar. "How did it happen?"

"Brandon says Pete was doing fine one minute, then he spaced out and mumbled something about his left arm aching, and next thing he'd nailed his hand."

"How far away are they?" Logan asked.

"Ten minutes. The McCaffrey place."

"I've been wanting to take a look at what Dylan and Olivia are building—want to drive over there?"

Maggie nodded, looking relieved. "Pete's a stubborn old bastard, but he's a great guy."

"Sounds like your typical Sloan." Logan turned to Clare. "You and Owen can help yourself to Gran's Dutch cocoa."

She nodded. "We'll be fine. If you need anything, let me know."

Logan grabbed his jacket and followed Maggie out the front door. She had driven her van to the house. "Easier to load books in the van," she said.

"We can take my car."

"Logan..." She inhaled deeply. "You're worried something more is wrong with Uncle Pete than a nail-gun accident, aren't you?"

"I'd like to check him out."

TWELVE

He had never dreamed that any walk—that any thing—could give him so much happiness.

—Charles Dickens, *A Christmas Carol*

CLARE FINISHED DECORATING THE TREE and enlisted Owen's help to stack the decoration boxes, glad there was plenty to do with Logan and Maggie checking on Pete Sloan. She had the ancient vacuum out when they returned an hour later. "How is he?" she asked, unwinding the heavy vacuum cord and flopping it onto the floor.

"He's on his way to the hospital," Logan said.

Maggie unzipped her jacket. "That's the understatement of the year. Our Dr. Farrell just saved Pete from a massive stroke or heart attack—whether tonight or a month from now, who knows. It's in the works. Logan also got through Pete's thick Sloan head that he needed to go to the ER and get checked out." She grinned suddenly. "That's the layman's version."

"It works," Logan said, shrugging off his jacket and tossing it on a chair. "Olivia and Dylan are building quite a place, but it blends in with the land out there. He seems excited about getting his adventure-travel business off the ground."

"Brandon's excited, too," Maggie said. "He's helping out part-time. He knows he needs to go in for regular physicals but today with his uncle will be a wakeup call. I don't want him nailing his hand twenty or thirty years from now because he refused to see a doctor. Not that I'm blaming Pete for having an accident, mind you, but if there are things you can do to stay healthy, I'm all for doing them."

"Pete's healthy," Logan said. "People make mistakes."

"Yeah. We're all human. That's why we have hospital emergency departments and doctors who specialize in emergency medicine." Maggie gasped, spinning around to Clare. "I'm sorry. I didn't mean—I can't believe I said that. It was terribly insensitive of me. I don't do well with blood and sickness. I never have. It obviously made me stupid."

Clare stepped back from the vacuum. "You're not stupid, and you're entitled to speak your mind. You don't have to tiptoe around me."

Maggie shuddered. "I'm still an idiot. You're nicer than I deserve."

"I very much doubt that."

Logan took the vacuum cord and plugged it into a socket.

"Look, I have to run," Maggie said. "Pete's accident ate up the free time I had. Rain check on the books?"

"Of course," Clare said.

"A mea culpa bottle of wine later?"

"I'll split a bottle of wine with you anytime, Maggie. It doesn't need to involve a mea culpa."

Maggie relaxed, clearly putting her faux pas behind her. She wasn't one to dwell on her mistakes, Clare thought. Recognize it, own it, apologize and move on. Maggie O'Dunn Sloan wasn't a ruminator. She turned to Logan. "Thank you for your help."

"Not a problem."

"Do you get many nail-gun accidents in Boston?"

"You'd be surprised."

"I guess I shouldn't be, since Brandon and I lived there for a few years. We love the city, but we decided to come back to Knights Bridge to raise our boys." She smiled, her turquoise eyes brightening. "That's the short version. See you both later."

She flew out the front door, racing down the steps and out to her van.

"Her energy amazes me," Clare said with a smile.

"She's had a jolt of adrenaline, too," Logan said. "I can do the vacuuming."

"Thanks. Owen's investigating the rest of the toy drawer in the dining room. I'll organize the books and stage the boxes for quick transport when I get a chance to bring them to the library."

"On second thought, vacuuming can wait and I can help you with the books." Logan stood straight, winking at her. "In my world, vacuuming can always wait."

Clare laughed. "Funny, I say the same thing."

They hauled the boxes out to the porch. Logan seemed tireless, and he showed no concern about what books were in the boxes. "Library's free to have them," he said. "I'm glad to have them put to good use. They'd just be collecting dust here."

"I have no idea what will sell," she said, following Logan down the stairs with a box. "Vera tells me there's no predicting. Have you ever been to one of the library's book sales?"

"I haven't, no."

She stood straight, brushing strands of stray hair out

of her face. "I'm looking forward to my first. It will include a bake sale."

Logan caught one last hair and tucked it behind her ear. "I have about two dozen of Gran's molasses cookies left," he said.

"They'd be a hit."

Justin Sloan pulled up in front of the house in his truck. From his look as he got out, Clare didn't think he was bringing bad news. He thumped up the porch steps. "Thought you'd want to know Pete's going to be fine. They're running some tests. He might need a stent or two, but most likely whatever's going on with him can be treated with medication." He nodded to Logan. "Thanks for stepping in."

"No problem. I appreciate the update, and I'm glad he's getting any underlying issues addressed."

Justin grunted. "He'd haunt me for sure if he died on the job."

The Sloan humor. Clare was still getting accustomed to it herself.

Logan grinned. "This town's filled with ghosts."

Justin grinned back at him. "Don't you forget it." He glanced around at the decorated porch. "The place looks good. You'd never know no one was living here. Let me know if you need help with anything." He pointed at the stack of boxes. "Getting rid of these?"

"They're books Daisy is donating to the library," Clare said.

"I'll give you a hand."

Having Justin's help would speed up the job. He suggested they use his truck to transport the books to the library. They had the boxes loaded into the back in a few trips. Neither man broke a sweat that Clare could see, but she didn't mind admitting she could feel perspiration on the back of her neck. She'd been running around since she'd gotten out of bed that morning. Owen was still playing in the dining room. He'd had a big couple of days and seemed to appreciate some quiet time.

"I'll unload the truck when I get to the library," Justin said as they stood on the sidewalk in front of the house. "Any particular place you want them?"

"By the stage would work," Clare said. "I can help—"

"I'll be done before you get there. My front seat's loaded with boxes of screws or I'd offer you a ride."

"Thank you, Justin."

He shrugged. "Anytime."

He climbed in his truck and was gone, heading up South Main the short distance to the library.

Clare turned to Logan. "I should get over there. I'll grab Owen. We can walk. I could use some air after decorating and hauling books."

"Why don't I walk with you? I could use some air, too."

"Because of the musty boxes and balsam fir needles or because of saving Pete Sloan with his nephews watching you?"

"Talk about pressure," Logan said with a grin, skimming a curved finger along her lower jaw. "I'd like to walk with you. That's all."

"You're looking for a way out of vacuuming balsam fir needles off the rug?"

"I never procrastinate."

"If I believe that, will you tell me next that Santa Claus is for real?"

"I don't know about Santa Claus, but Dickens' Christmas ghosts damn sure are for real."

"Another one paid you a visit?"

"Marley. Scary old bastard. At least it wasn't one of the Christmas spirits."

Owen wasn't thrilled about taking a walk but he got into it once he found out they were going to the library. When they started up South Main, sunlight was sparkling on the snow on the common and in yards. A fresh dusting from last night added to the winter-wonderland quality of Knights Bridge village. Clare couldn't imagine a prettier place to spend Christmas.

When they reached the library, Justin Sloan was carrying the last box of books up the steps. Not a man to waste time. He set it in the entry, muttered he had to get rolling and climbed back in his truck, waving as he shut the door and drove off.

Owen raced into the children's room. The library wasn't open—Clare hadn't even thought about giving Justin a key, but he obviously had one. Another thing she had to figure out: who had keys to the place.

Logan pulled the smallest box off the top of the stack and opened it.

"Well, I'll be damned," he said half under his breath, holding up an old edition of *A Christmas Carol*. "I swear I'm being haunted."

Clare laughed, but when he handed her the book, she saw that it was a *very* old edition. She opened it, and a yellowed, folded note fell out. She caught it and handed it to Logan.

He unfolded it. She saw his eyes tear up when he read it. He obviously couldn't speak and handed it to her. The handwriting wasn't neat, but it was legible.

Christmas Day, 1945

To Daisy,
I will always remember my Christmases past with Angus, but I am glad we're together this Christ-

mas. I hope we will be together for many Christmases yet to come.

Tom

"That's so sweet," Clare said. "Who is Angus?"

"My great-uncle. Angus Farrell."

"Your grandfather's older brother who was killed in
World War II?"

Logan nodded and tucked the note back into the
book. "My grandfather never talked about him. Not to
me." He cleared his throat. "And I never asked."

"This book obviously meant something to your
grandfather, and probably to your grandmother, too."

"It could be a valuable edition, couldn't it?"

"Possibly. George Sanderson donated his book collection to the library. It contained some rare books. This
could have been one of them, only no one realized it
and it went into one of the library sales. They've been
going on for decades."

Logan shut the book. "Let's go see my grandmother.
Would you join me?"

"It's library business. Part of its history."

"I meant for my sake," he said quietly.

They dropped Owen off with Maggie and drove out
to Rivendell in Logan's car.

Daisy was awake, watching her favorite soap opera and doing a crossword puzzle, relaxing after a senior yoga class with Audrey Frost. "You should see Grace doing the cobra, and she's even older than I am."

Logan smiled. "Nice and limber now, Gran?"

"I feel good, whatever the reason."

"We were going through books and found this one." He handed her the copy of *A Christmas Carol*.

"Oh, my. I knew it was there somewhere. Tom..." She smiled, touching the worn cover with her age-spotted hands. "He was late with a book report on Charles Dickens and chose to read this because it was short."

"Gran, he mentions his brother," Logan said. "Does what happened to Angus have something to do with the candle?"

"Have a seat. I'll tell you."

THIRTEEN

➤←

"Men's courses will foreshadow certain ends,
to which, if persevered in, they must lead,"
said Scrooge. "But if the courses be departed from,
the ends will change."

–CHARLES DICKENS, *A CHRISTMAS CAROL*

December, 1945

AFTER TOM'S VISIT WITH THE CANDLE, DAISY'S
father relented about decorating the house for Christmas
and apologized to her and her mother for being such a
Scrooge. He drove them out to the Farrell farm, on Tom's
invitation, and they collected pinecones and princess pine.
At home, they found a bit of red ribbon and made a simple

wreath. But Daisy could tell her father still didn't have his heart in Christmas.

After church on Christmas Eve, she placed Tom's candle on a small, flat stone in the living room window and lit the blackened wick. Her father sat in his chair by the fire and stared at the flame, not saying a word.

Daisy was about to head upstairs to bed when she heard singing.

She went to a window and peered out into the darkness, and she could see Tom, his father and a dozen carolers from town gathered in front of the house, each holding a small, lit candle.

They sang "Silent Night."

Her father got up from his chair. Her mother wandered in from the kitchen. He put his arm around her, and they stood at the window where Tom's candle burned.

Daisy wasn't sure they noticed her slip outside. She wasn't wearing a coat but didn't notice the cold as she eased next to Tom. She joined in, singing "White Christmas," although she wasn't sure she hit any of the right notes. To her surprise, Tom hit all the notes. He had a deep, beautiful voice.

When the song ended and carolers started on to the next house, he squeezed her hand. "Merry Christmas, Daisy," he said, kissing her on the cheek.

It wasn't until after Tom and the rest of the carolers had gone that his mother came to the house. Daisy's father was the first to notice Betty Farrell standing outside, alone. Daisy went out with him, but he asked her to stay on the porch.

"It's just a candle," Betty said when he stood next to her. "It'll burn out."

He put an arm around her. "It's been hard coming home when so many others didn't. I've felt…guilty. This candle—Betty, I know…I *know* it made a difference to your son."

"I miss him."

"Like no one else can."

She stared at the burning candle in the window. "I'm glad you came home safe. We can't live in the past, you and I, but I think of Angus…" Her voice faltered. "He loved Christmas."

"I remember, Betty."

"It's almost Christmas Day. We're on our way to midnight service at church. Keep the candle, won't you? Burn it every Christmas Eve, for as long as it lasts. Then when it's gone…" She bit on her lower lip and didn't continue.

"We'll make another," Tom said, walking across from the common, joining his mother. "Better yet, buy one.

You almost burned down the house making the last batch of candles. Hot wax is highly flammable."

"Go on with you, Tom."

Daisy walked down from the porch and stood beside her father as they watched Betty Farrell and her surviving son walk across the common together. *I'm going to marry Tom Farrell one day*, she thought.

Then she noticed her father looking at her, and she wondered if she'd thought aloud. But he smiled at her, kissed her on the top of the head and went inside with her.

They kept the candle burning until the stroke of midnight, then blew it out, until the next Christmas Eve.

Present day

When Daisy finished her story, she was aware the room had gone silent. She noticed with shock the deep lines and brown spots on her hands. For a moment, she'd been fifteen again, falling in love with a boy who missed his brother lost to war, and always would.

She touched the simple cover of *A Christmas Carol* in her lap. "Tom gave me this book on Christmas Day. He said he bought it at a library sale. He was so pleased with himself." She smiled up at her grandson. "He said we helped him and his mother think about Christmases yet to come, and not just Christmases past."

"Gran." Logan was having difficulty speaking. "I knew he'd lost a brother in the war, but I never—I've never considered what it must have been like for him and his family, or for you."

"Angus was killed in Holland in September, 1944. He was the only serviceman from Knights Bridge who was killed in the war, but the Farrells weren't alone. So many people lost loved ones. It's easy to forget that the names on war monuments are of real people."

"And the candle we found," Clare said. "It's the one your mother-in-law made?"

Daisy nodded. "Tom and I continued the tradition of lighting a candle in the front window at Christmas. We kept that one going for a few years, but he got to where he thought it would set the house on fire, it was so old. I didn't realize he'd saved it, or if I did, I forgot. He was usually so unsentimental."

"It was in its own box inside another box," Logan said.

"The book was in a small box, too," Clare said. "It's obviously a family heirloom that wasn't intended for the sale."

Daisy touched a finger to the gold lettering on the cover. "Our first real conversation was over Tom's book report on *A Christmas Carol*. He wasn't much of a student." She cleared her throat, looked up at the two young people. "We had a good life together. He loved you so much, Logan. Angus was a medic. I think he'd have been a doctor if he could have, but he planned to come back to the farm."

"Did he leave behind a girlfriend or a fiancée?" Logan asked.

"We always thought he was sweet on Grace Webster."

Grace, who'd been living with a secret only recently revealed to anyone else in town. Had Angus guessed? Daisy hadn't asked Grace, and never would. She looked at Clare. "Tom loved buying books and then donating them to the library after we'd read them, but I was a pack rat and kept a lot of them."

Clare nodded, but she was breathing rapidly, overcome with emotion.

Daisy hadn't expected that. "Are you all right?" she asked the young woman.

Another nod. "I should get going. Owen and I…" She waved a hand toward the door. "We have a few errands we need to do."

"I hope I didn't upset you," Daisy said, alarmed.

"No, no. I'm fine. Thank you for telling your story. Having me here."

"Your husband—he wasn't in the military, was he?"

Clare shook her head. "He died in a car accident," she

mumbled, then pointed again, vaguely. "I'll go now. I'll find my way back to town. Thank you both."

"Cookies," Logan said, jumping up. "It's time for molasses cookies. I swear I'm never going to run out. Gran, you okay—"

"I'll be fine sitting right here."

She handed him the book. He was already on the move. That was Logan, she thought affectionately, sinking into her chair. She closed her eyes, remembering when Tom Farrell knocked on her front door on Christmas Day during her senior year in high school. He wanted to take her ice-skating on Echo Lake. He had graduated and was already a firefighter, and it was their first real date…but she'd been in love with him since he'd helped turn her father away from bitterness and his mother away from sadness and loss by the simple act of lighting a candle.

It was reading *A Christmas Carol* with its transformation of Ebenezer Scrooge that had given him the idea— and the courage—to bring the candle into town and see what he could do.

I hated every second of writing that book report, though.

Daisy smiled at the memory. He'd always expected to go first and had wanted her to be ready, but how could she ever be ready?

She got up, slowly, carefully, and headed into the hall, figuring she'd run into someone she knew.

Grace was in the sunroom, watching her birds and reading a book.

"Do you remember Angus Farrell?" Daisy asked, sitting in a chair next to her longtime friend.

"Angus? Of course. He was so full of life…" Grace sighed. "I don't think any of us ever imagined he wouldn't survive the war. Of all those who went, Angus seemed one of the most likely to come home."

"Tom's mother used to fantasize Angus was wandering around Belgium or Holland with a head injury and couldn't remember who he was."

"But you and Tom visited his grave, didn't you?"

"In Holland, yes. His mother had died by then. She knew Angus had been killed. Picturing him drinking beer at a Dutch café was a little fantasy she allowed herself sometimes."

Grace seemed unconvinced. "I suppose."

Daisy smiled. "You've always had your feet firmly planted in reality, haven't you, Grace?"

"This you ask of someone rereading *The Scarlet Pimpernel* for at least the twentieth time." She pointed at the feeders. "It's quiet today. Let's sit a moment, shall we, and see if our cardinal shows up?"

A Recipe for Hot Chocolate

⟶ ⟵

⅓ cup Droste or other cocoa (unsweetened)
½ cup sugar (or to taste)
⅓ cup hot water
4 cups milk
½ teaspoon vanilla extract (optional)

Combine cocoa and sugar in a medium saucepan. Blend in water. Stirring constantly, cook over medium heat until mixture comes to a boil. Let boil, continuing to stir, for two minutes. Add milk, heat to desired temperature (don't boil). Remove from heat and add vanilla. Serve by itself or topped with whipped cream and/or marshmallows.

FOURTEEN

Really, for a man who had been out of practice
for so many years, it was a splendid laugh,
a most illustrious laugh.

–CHARLES DICKENS, *A CHRISTMAS CAROL*

MOLASSES COOKIES AND MILK IN DAISY'S
kitchen did the trick. Clare felt better. "It's not kale,"
she said with a smile. "It's a good source of calcium."

Logan shuddered. "There are dark green leafy vegetables, and there's kale."

"Not your favorite?"

"I don't even want to think about it while I'm eating
a molasses cookie."

She laughed, enjoying his company, but she knew his mind was on his grandmother's story.

"I have to get rolling," he said. "I have a twelve-hour overnight shift and need to get myself ready. Keep the key to the house. Check for more books, drop by for cookies with Owen—my house is your house."

"You say that now. Wait until I eat all the cookies."

He kissed her softly. "We can always make more cookies."

"I'm going to find out more about your grandmother's edition of *A Christmas Carol*."

"I've only seen the movie adaptations. I've never read the book."

"What's your favorite adaptation?"

"I'm not sure I have a particular favorite. Maybe we can watch different versions together."

"Logan…"

He pressed a finger to her lips. "No thinking right now. Not with molasses, sugar and butter in your system."

Not to mention him, she thought. "Have a good shift at the hospital."

She returned to the library after he left. Daisy's books were a temptation, but she got the boxes out of the way. She didn't expect to find anything else as intriguing and potentially valuable as *A Christmas Carol*. The small library was different from what she was accustomed to in Boston, but she loved its atmosphere and the breadth of the work she did. She had no ambitions beyond doing the best job she could and making a home for herself and Owen.

When she picked him up at the Sloans' house, Owen wanted Logan to come back to their sawmill apartment with them. Clare explained he'd returned to Boston to work. Owen looked thoughtful for a moment. "Logan'll be back. He likes it here."

"Do you like it here, Owen?"

He beamed. "I *love* it here. In Knights Bridge," he added quickly as they went up to their apartment. "You still need your own room, Mom. And I want to live in a house next to Aidan and Tyler so we can walk to school together. You could walk to the library. What about Logan's house? Tyler says it's for sale. Can we buy it?"

"We won't be living in this place forever, but it's good right now. It's quiet."

"I can hear the waterfall."

"How many places have their own waterfall?"

He liked that. His transition from city life to country life hadn't been without incident, but he was making friends, doing well in school and seemed content.

He plugged in the lights on their Charlie Brown Christmas tree and crawled under a blanket on the couch, yawning as Clare read him a story. After he went to bed, she kept the tree lights on as she tried to hear the water tumbling over the dam, rocks and ice, and imagine Logan with her.

On Tuesday, Clare drove into Boston for a workshop at a city college for small-town librarians. While she was in town, she stopped to see a friend, an archivist and rare books specialist. It was enough to prompt her to walk over to the busy hospital where Logan worked, but she also wanted to see it for herself.

The emergency department was relatively quiet at four o'clock on a December weekday afternoon. She didn't want to interrupt Logan—wasn't sure he was there—but she appreciated seeing where he spent his days, and, often, his nights. His life was so different from hers. Even when she had lived in Boston, she'd had a quiet work life compared to his. What had drawn him into emergency medicine?

She hadn't been in an emergency room since Stephen's death.

"Clare," Logan said behind her.

She turned, smiling at him. "You caught me. I hope I'm not disturbing you."

"Not at all." He wore a suit under a white doctor's coat, his eyes on her as they stepped away from the desk.

"I've been deep in documentation. It's not the most exciting part of my job but it has to be done."

"You don't do well with tedious tasks."

"Ah. You *are* getting to know me."

"I won't keep you. I'm in town on library business, but I wanted to tell you that it looks as if the edition of *A Christmas Carol* your grandfather gave to your grandmother could be a first edition. I recommend having it appraised."

"It belongs to the library now."

"It wouldn't be right to keep it."

"Someone made a mistake putting it into the book sale when my grandfather bought it. Gran obviously wanted the library to have it back. She doesn't need to sell it for the money. What makes you think it's a first edition?"

"A friend who knows about such things told me. It was first published in 1843 by Chapman & Hall in England, with a pink-brown cloth cover and gold lettering. That first edition had green endpapers, but the ink wasn't fast and came off on people's fingers—so it was changed in subsequent editions to yellow."

"And Gran's copy has green endpapers?"

Clare nodded. "The yellow would be valuable, too. The etchings and engravings also suggest a first edition. The book was an instant bestseller. Dickens was very involved in its publication. It was his idea to sell it at a low five shillings per copy."

"That must have helped," Logan said. "I'll be happy to have it appraised, but it belongs at the library. It would be a great annual Christmas display."

"I wish we had a copy of your grandfather's book report."

"I wouldn't be surprised if Gran saved it, but I bet he burned it before she got the chance. Speaking of Christmas, I am free as of 7:00 a.m. on Christmas Eve and I have Christmas Day off. I've decided to spend it in Knights Bridge. I did promise Gran I'd light a candle in the window." He fell silent, as if taking pause to remember Daisy's story about her father and brother-in-law. Finally he stood straight, the busy ER doctor again. "What are your plans for Christmas?"

"I don't know about Christmas Eve yet, except for the early service at church with Owen. I imagine he'll get me up early on Christmas Day. Santa has big plans for him. Well…maybe not quite as big as Owen thinks."

"Let me make dinner for you two on Christmas Eve."

"That would be lovely, thank you."

An ambulance arrived. Logan clearly had to go. Clare left him to his work and went back to hers. As she left through a revolving door, she was breathing rapidly, but her mind was on the future, not the past.

★ ★ ★

Four hours after Clare left the hospital, Logan finally had time to grab a sandwich and sit for a few minutes. His visit with her was a blur, but he knew he'd said he'd be spending Christmas Eve in Knights Bridge and invited her to his grandmother's house for dinner.

"Christmas Eve in Knights Bridge?" His friend Paul chuckled over a beer together that evening. "Great. You can catch up on your sleep."

"I'll need a week of Christmas Eves in Knights Bridge to catch up on my sleep."

"I hear you. What's drawing you to your dad's hometown?"

"My grandmother."

"She's lived there for eighty-plus years. Damn, Logan. You've never had this look when you've mentioned the Farrell hometown."

Logan frowned. "What look?"

"Twitchy."

"Twitchy isn't a look."

"With you it is. Your grandmother's great. I met her, remember? She came to town with a cake and that insane fruit salad with the coconut. That was the best. I think it had almonds in it, too."

"Pecans." Logan yawned. "I'm calling it a night."

His friend leaned back, eyes narrowed, appraising. "It's the librarian."

"Good night, Paul."

"I admit my mind flooded with stereotypes when I heard a librarian had shown up at the hospital to see you, but I caught a peek of her. Pretty, pretty. A little on the harried side, and she obviously doesn't like hospitals. I can't say I blame her. *I* don't like hospitals. She looked like she wanted to throw up—I take it that wasn't you."

"Her husband died in an ER."

"Ouch. Not ours, I hope?"

"I don't know which one. Boston, somewhere. She was expecting."

His friend blinked in confusion. "Expecting what? Her husband to come home for dinner?"

"A baby, Paul."

"She was *pregnant?* Double ouch."

"She had a baby boy. Owen. He's six now. Cute kid. We cut a Christmas tree together."

"Logan…" Paul was serious now. "Being back in Boston hasn't helped you snap back to your senses?"

"Not yet."

"Volunteer for a double shift. A triple shift. Anything."

"I don't need to. I'm visited by Ebenezer Scrooge's ghosts at night. They're trying to get me to change my approach to Christmas, maybe to life."

"They only visit when you're in Knights Bridge, right? Not here in Boston."

"Here as well as at home."

"Home." Paul grimaced, finishing his beer. "Logan."

"Did I just call Knights Bridge home? Damn. It's been a long day."

"It's a cute town. A picnic on the town common, a stroll in the shade—"

"There's a skating rink on the common in winter."

"I hate ice-skating. I got ten stitches once when my brother tripped me. He says it was an accident. I don't believe him." Paul shrugged. "Okay, maybe it was a couple of Band-Aids but it felt like stitches. Loads of blood. I think I decided to go into medicine then."

"You loved it," Logan said, amused. "You felt like a hockey player."

"Dylan McCaffrey lives in Knights Bridge now. He was a hell of a hockey player. I hear he's made a fortune since then."

"Let's change the subject."

The temperature had dropped when Logan headed back to his apartment. He hit a wind tunnel, a gust of frigid air slamming into him. He half expected one of Scrooge's Christmas ghosts to ooze out of the shadows. Old Ebenezer had most feared the Ghost of Christmas Yet to Come. *Do I fear him?* Logan asked himself. Would he become a workaholic doctor with a string of divorces and estranged children? Would he face burnout alone and bitter?

And Clare Morgan. She was content with her life in Knights Bridge, but she was lonely. What would the Ghost of Christmas Yet to Come show her?

Logan shook off such thinking. He buttoned his jacket and walked faster. He hadn't planned anything special for Christmas before deciding to go to Knights Bridge. Work, a movie, sleep. He'd have called his family and not thought twice about the kind of life he was leading. His ability to shut out everything and focus on the present was an asset in emergency medicine. He could be impatient and irritable but he didn't have a noisy mind.

Did that make him shallow, destined to live an unexamined life?

He thought of his grandfather's note to his grandmother. The love—the depth of that love.

He crossed Boylston Street, glad to be out of the wind. He walked down to the tall, beautifully lit Christmas tree outside the Prudential Center. A long day at work and a good evening with a friend, but he thought of how much Owen Morgan would enjoy the tree…and Clare.

Logan shut his eyes, but it was as if she were here with him, with her smile, with her translucent skin, pale hair and shapely body.

He gritted his teeth. He was an idiot.

He needed to go home, get some sleep, go to work tomorrow and regroup.

And plan Christmas Eve dinner.

FIFTEEN

>+<

"I am as light as a feather, I am as happy
as an angel, I am as merry as a school-boy.
I am as giddy as a drunken man.
A merry Christmas to everybody!"

—CHARLES DICKENS, *A CHRISTMAS CAROL*

LOGAN HAD CHRISTMAS EVE LUNCH WITH
his grandmother and her friends in the Rivendell dining
room. Clare saw him laughing with the white-haired
women as she dropped off books. She didn't interrupt
them, just left quietly and returned to the library.

Owen, Aidan and Tyler Sloan, and a handful of other
children arrived for story hour.

It was snowing lightly when she closed the library and

she and Owen walked down South Main Street toward the Farrell house.

"That's Logan," Owen said, pointing across the street at a man on the common.

Logan waved to them. Clare took Owen's hand and ran across the street with him.

"I want to show you something," Logan said.

They walked to the town's World War II memorial. Carved in the granite were names of Knights Bridge men who'd served during the war, and the one who'd died?

Angus Robert Farrell.

Logan touched his great-uncle's name. "I found a picture of him at the house."

"He looked a lot like you," Clare said.

"The librarian at work?"

"I found a notice about him…"

"His obituary," Logan said. "He died during Operation Market Garden. It was a long time ago to us. To the women I had lunch with, it must feel like yesterday."

"I'm glad Daisy told you the story about the candle."

"I am, too." He looked up at the gray sky, the snow easing. Then he turned to Clare and took her hand. "What do you say the three of us go ice-skating before dinner?"

Owen was all for it. Clare couldn't remember the last time she'd been on skates, but she realized she was excited about the idea. And he'd obviously been planning it, since he'd borrowed skates for her from Maggie Sloan.

With Dylan McCaffrey and Olivia Frost's Christmas Eve wedding, the skating rink was quiet. Logan glided out onto the ice with Owen as Clare got used to being on skates again.

"It's like riding a bike," she said, laughing as she eased onto the ice.

Owen found a stray hockey puck and hockey stick and busied himself pretending he was an NHL player. Logan eased in next to Clare, sweeping an arm around her and spinning her out onto the ice.

The snow picked up again, glowing in the Christmas lights as dusk descended on the village.

When they finally crossed South Main Street to the Farrell house, it was almost dark. Logan had the dining room table set for dinner and a sweet-potato-and-apple casserole, baked salmon with chive-and-parsley butter, green beans and rolls set to go.

"Dessert's hot chocolate and marshmallows," he said. "I'm not much on baking."

After dinner, they went into the front room. A fire burned in the fireplace, and the Christmas tree twinkled with its strings of lights. Logan set the half-melted pillar candle on the windowsill—the same candle Betty Farrell, his great-grandmother, had made in her farmhouse kitchen and lit on Christmas Eve through the war that had claimed her older son.

He got the candle lit just as carolers arrived in front of the house.

Clare took his hand. "Come on. Let's join them."

The snow had stopped, just an inch or so freshening up the landscape. Pleased to have a six-year-old in their midst, the carolers asked Owen what he would like to sing. "'Jingle Bells,'" he said happily, then smiled up at Logan and his mother. "This is going to be the best Christmas ever."

And so it would be, Clare thought, feeling Logan's arm come around her and realizing that she was in love with him.

A Recipe for Baked Sweet Potatoes and Apples

→ ←

*Sweet potatoes, apples, butter and apple cider are
all handy staples. Combined, they're irresistible.
Old-fashioned cider mills like the one Justin Sloan plans
to renovate dot the New England countryside. Some are
still in use, producing fresh apple cider.*

3 medium sweet potatoes
2 apples
¾ cup apple cider
4 tablespoons butter, cut in pieces

1. Preheat oven to 350°F. Parboil sweet potatoes, then drain,
   cool, peel and slice about ¼" thick into buttered casserole,
   alternating with apples, also sliced about ¼" thick. Pour
   cider over all and dot with butter. Bake until apples and
   sweet potatoes are soft, about 45 minutes.

2. For added sweetness, add about ½ cup of brown sugar to the
   cider. For added spiciness, add ½ teaspoon each of ground
   nutmeg and allspice to the cider.

A Recipe for Chive-and-Parsley Butter

Chives and parsley are easy to grow in pots through the winter, and fresh herbs are readily available in supermarkets. Herb butters have many uses, from adding to mashed potatoes to melting atop grilled or baked salmon.

1 cup unsalted butter
1 teaspoon salt (optional)
2 tablespoons chopped fresh chives
2 tablespoons chopped fresh parsley

Mix all ingredients together and chill for at least 2 hours to blend flavors. May be frozen for up to a month.

EPILOGUE

... And it was always said of him, that he knew
how to keep Christmas well, if any man alive
possessed the knowledge. May that be truly
said of us, and all of us!

—Charles Dickens, *A Christmas Carol*

Almost four months later

APRIL SHOWERS MIGHT BRING MAY FLOW-
ers, Logan thought, but they also brought mud. He'd at
least had the sense to change into his running shoes before leaving Boston. His emergency department had dealt
with a mass casualty incident—a multiple-car pileup on
Storrow Drive—and he was bone tired. But he couldn't

imagine anywhere he wanted to be more than Knights Bridge.

He entered his grandmother's house. The Christmas decorations were long put away, and the tree and boughs ground up for mulch. He could continue to divide his time between here and Boston, but he had options in emergency medicine closer to Knights Bridge.

Closer to home.

Clare would be at the library, getting ready for the spring book sale. The appraisal of *A Christmas Carol* had come back, and it was, indeed, a first edition. It almost certainly had come from George Sanderson's collection. It was worth a great deal, and it helped that Tom Farrell had written his note to his sweetheart separately and not on the pages of the old copy of the Dickens classic he'd grabbed for his book report.

He smiled when he went into the front room and discovered stacks of swatches and paint chips on the coffee table. Clare's doing, with the help of her Knights Bridge friends. The house wasn't going on the market. It was staying in the Farrell family, and he couldn't be more pleased—but no one was happier than Daisy Farrell.

The place needed infrastructure work—a new furnace, updated wiring, a new roof—but Clare was far more interested in the cosmetic changes. In addition to her friends, she was getting advice from Daisy, Audrey, Grace and a few other elderly women at Rivendell. There was a lot of wisdom in that facility, if also a lot of wrinkles.

Logan was staying out of the decorating. Clare could decide to paint every room purple and he wouldn't care.

Well, maybe purple would be going too far.

He had hired Mark Flanagan, the local architect married to Randy and Louise Frost's younger daughter. Logan wasn't worried about extensive work on the house getting started. He and Clare would have her little sawmill apartment when needed.

He had it all planned out in his head, this new life of his.

But when he heard Clare running up the porch steps, he realized his palms were sweating and his heart was beating rapidly, a rarity for him even during his medical school days.

She came inside, smiling as she greeted him.

"Marry me," he said. "Clare… Clare, Clare, Clare. I love you. I had this big speech planned, but that's all there is to it. I love you, and I want you to be my wife."

She put her hand over her mouth, clearly speechless.

They'd declared their love numerous times since Christmas, but this was different. This wasn't just about sex and the emotions of the moment. This was about commitment. About their lives together.

And about Owen. The little boy was already lobbying for a little sister or brother.

Clare and I can make that happen, Logan thought.

He took her fingers into his and kissed them. "Let's try that again. Clare Morgan, will you marry me?"

She nodded, tears in her eyes. "Yes, Logan Farrell, I will marry you." She slipped her arms around him. "I love you. I love you so much."

Clare had promised to help Maggie lead a candle-making workshop at Rivendell. The story of Daisy's candle had inspired the seniors. Logan just hoped they didn't set the place on fire, but they'd taken proper precautions.

Daisy and her friends had gathered in a small meeting room, and Maggie had set up for the workshop. Instead of seeing geriatric issues—aging organs, forgetfulness, chronic disease—Logan focused on the smiles and laughter. The past, present and future had come together in that small room.

He stood back as Clare, confident and still a bit red-cheeked from his proposal, announced that she and Logan were engaged. No one seemed surprised, only happy. Love and weddings were in the air lately in Knights Bridge.

As they got on with their candle making, Logan swore

he saw the Farrell brothers laughing in the corner, together again as they watched the girls they'd loved, now old women.

But maybe it was just the spring sunshine and shadows.

The nub of a candle was still in the front window on South Main. It had been his idea to leave it there. He and Clare would light it tonight, one last time before they had new candles to light.

His eyes connected with hers, and she smiled. He smiled back, with a love that would take them through many Christmases yet to come…and was forever.

★ ★ ★ ★ ★

AUTHOR NOTE

EVERY DECEMBER, WE WATCH *A CHRISTMAS Carol*. There are many great adaptations, but our favorite is the 1951 version with Alastair Sim as Scrooge. But we also love the Muppet version. Who can forget Rizzo the Rat?

Candles are a big part of our Christmas celebrations, but we leave the candle making to others. I remember one Christmas when the power went out, and we gathered around the woodstove to stay warm and lit candles as we sang carols.

A Knights Bridge Christmas is part of my Swift River Valley series. The story takes place the same Christmas as Olivia Frost and Dylan McCaffrey's wedding, which is featured in my enovella, *Christmas at Carriage Hill*. It is also the same winter that Heather Sloan meets her match in Brody Hancock in *Echo Lake*. In my upcoming *The Spring at Moss Hill*, reclusive Kylie Shaw has a secret that relentless private investigator Russ Colton is determined to find out.

For more information about the Swift River Valley series and all my books, please visit my website and sign up for my newsletter, and join me on Facebook and Twitter. Merry Christmas!

Carla
www.carlaneggers.com